THE CUPID CRAWL

A WILLIAMSVILLE INN STORY

HANK EDWARDS

STARTLED MONKEYS MEDIA

This is a work of fiction. Names, characters, businesses, places, events and incidents are either the products of the author's imagination or used in a fictitious manner. Any resemblance to actual persons, living or dead, or actual events is purely coincidental.

The Cupid Crawl ©2020 Hank Edwards
Cover design by Brigham Vaughn
Book design and production by Hank Edwards
Editing by Deanna Wadsworth

All rights reserved. This book or any portion thereof may not be reproduced or used in any manner whatsoever without the express written permission of the publisher except for the use of brief quotations in a book review.

Printed in the United States of America

First Publication, 2020

CONTENTS

Chapter 1	1
Chapter 2	8
Chapter 3	14
Chapter 4	21
Chapter 5	31
Chapter 6	40
Chapter 7	59
Chapter 8	74
Chapter 9	88
Chapter 10	105
Chapter 11	124
Chapter 12	136
Chapter 13	145
Chapter 14	164
About the Author	183
Also by Hank Edwards	185

CHAPTER ONE

"Stop pulling so hard, you're going to stretch it out."

"I bet you don't say that to Rex," Carter said as he stepped back.

Will stopped struggling and turned to face him. Or, rather, he turned his body in the direction of Carter's voice, his face covered by a too-tight sweater that wouldn't pull down over his head. Carter smirked and shook his head as he looked fondly at his best friend.

"Stop smirking like that," Will said.

"You can't even see my face," Carter replied. "What makes you think I'm smirking?"

"Because I know you."

"Fair point," Carter said.

Will struggled a little longer, his arms trapped in an awkward raised position that made him look like he was half-heartedly trying to surrender. He finally gave up with a heavy sigh and bent at the waist, extending his arms toward Carter.

"Can you pull it off please? I'm getting claustrophobic in here."

"Not sure I feel comfortable pulling you off now that you're a married man—"

"Pull the sweater off," Will said, the volume of his voice going up and his tone edging close to anxious. "You know what I mean."

"Oh, of course," Carter said, and stepped forward.

He grabbed the sleeves of the sweater and stripped the garment off Will in one yank, the motion producing a barrage of popping and snapping from static electricity. Carter tossed the sweater onto the bed as Will straightened up and looked at him, his face red and hair standing out all over his head.

"Thank you," Will said with a nod.

"You're welcome," Carter said. "That sweater is a death trap. And I think you might have sent a power surge through your building."

Will grinned as he smoothed wrinkles from his static-ridden white undershirt and ran a hand through his hair. "Maybe it charged my phone battery?"

"Anything's possible."

Carter flopped onto bed and lounged across the mattress, toying with the sleeves of the discarded sweater as he watched Will go through the clothes hanging in his closet. Will was by far the best friend Carter ever had. Years ago, a mutual friend had introduced them, and Carter, being the more outgoing, had pretty much forced Will to go out. They'd dated for two weeks, and while the sex was enjoyable for both of them, they'd realized they fit better together as friends. It was a realization Carter was continuously grateful for.

"I never have anything to wear to these events," Will grumbled.

"Ah, the price of marrying into fame," Carter said with an elaborate sigh.

Will glanced over his shoulder at him. "You sound jealous."

"Envious, Big Willie. It's envy you hear." He rolled on his

back and stared at the ceiling fan. "Last year, you left me here in Boston to scamper off on a business trip to Nowheresville, Montana—"

"Williamsville, New York," Will corrected automatically without turning away from the closet. "And I have never scampered in my entire life. Ever."

Carter continued as if he hadn't been interrupted. "And you lived a storybook gay romance that ended up with you marrying one of the most eligible gay bachelors around."

Will looked over his shoulder. "You really think Rex was a most eligible gay bachelor?"

Carter fixed him with a raised-eyebrows look. "You don't?"

The blush that crept into Will's face was adorable, and a surge of joy swept through Carter. Joy tempered just a touch with envy. A little more than a year prior, in the weeks before Christmas, Will had gone on a business trip to Williamsville, New York, and stayed in a place called the Williamsville Inn. Across the snow-filled courtyard from Will's room, up-and-coming, out-and-proud gay singer, Rex Garland, had been trying to write a Christmas song with very little luck. Will overheard Rex's struggles and left lyric suggestions in a series of secret notes on the patio of Rex's hotel room. Eventually, the two met face-to-face and dated for a year. On this past New Year's Eve, Will and Rex were married, and now, five weeks later, Will was traveling with Rex to some event honoring out and visible gay artists from a variety of art forms.

While Carter was happy for his friend, he couldn't help wondering when his own life might go through a similar change. It wasn't that he was unhappy. Well, not really. Lonely would be a more appropriate description than unhappy. Deep down he knew he had no one to blame but himself. His excessive use of Grindr had gotten him to this point. The freedom and lack of commitment that accompanied the hookups had been nice, at first. But lately, Carter couldn't help missing something more substantial that a Grindr date couldn't provide.

"How about this?"

Will's question pulled Carter out of his musing and back to the moment. He assessed the blue Oxford that perfectly matched Will's eyes and provided a nice compliment to his dark blond beard.

"It's perfect," Carter said with a smile.

"Yeah?" Will held the shirt up and looked it over before nodding once. "Okay. Good. My top half is figured out."

He returned the shirt to the closet. "Now I need to find a pair of pants to go with it."

Carter sighed and got up. He took Will's arm, leading him to the end of the bed and gently sitting him on the edge of the mattress. Returning to the closet, Carter quickly assessed his friend's clothes, choosing a pair of black wool pants with blue pinstripes he'd forced Will to buy the year before. He hung those alongside the blue Oxford before selecting three more shirts and another two pairs of pants. For a final touch, he pulled a shiny gold bowtie off a hanger and draped it over the shoulder of the blue Oxford.

Stepping back, Carter gestured toward the closet. "Ta-da."

Remaining seated, Will gave him a beseeching look. "Permission to approach the clothes, your honor?"

Carter nodded once. "Permission granted."

Will stood and inspected the outfits, running his fingers along each item to feel the material. He smiled at Carter. "Thanks, Cartier."

The nickname Will had bestowed early in their relationship never failed to send a flutter of platonic warmth through him. "You're more than welcome, Big Willie. Can't have you looking like a mess on the red carpet."

"Ugh, red carpet." Will shook his head. "I can't believe I have to walk up a red carpet and be photographed."

"Oh no, how awful," Carter said with zero sympathy.

"Hey, I'm not an extrovert like you. Something like that is way outside of my comfort zone."

"It's good to stretch your boundaries once in a while. Just make sure there's a safe word involved."

Will chuckled, then turned serious. "Do you think I should come up with a safe word to let Rex know I need to escape for a little while and catch my breath?"

Carter nodded. "That's a good idea. How about 'man rammer'?"

Will frowned. "You're making fun of me."

"Am not."

"Are too."

"Am not."

"Are too!" Will exclaimed. "This is serious. You know I have self-esteem issues, and as great as Rex has been the past year, I'm kind of freaked out about all of this."

"I understand that, but I wasn't making fun of you," Carter said. "A safe word should be something you wouldn't say in the situation. When you're on the red carpet and hobnobbing with other musician types, do you think you'll spout off the phrase 'man rammer' at any time?"

"No, but—"

"Then that, or something like it, will definitely work. Plus it might give you both a moment of brevity during a stressful time."

Will looked at him in silence a moment, slowly stroking his full beard. "Your explanation makes sense, but the phrase seems a bit much."

Carter held his arms out to either side and smiled. "That should not surprise you."

Will cocked an eyebrow. "It doesn't." He suddenly strode across the room and gathered Carter into a tight hug. "Thank you. I don't know how I would have gotten through this past year without you."

Carter hugged Will tight and closed his eyes, savoring the closeness. He didn't want for physical contact—he got plenty of that through Grindr—but this was leaps and bounds different from that kind of contact. This was more personal than the hottest, sweatiest sex Carter had experienced. Will's simple hug was more intimate than any of those sexcapades, and it satisfied some quiet need inside him, even while it awakened another, deeper craving.

"I'm sure you would have muddled through somehow," Carter muttered.

"Not even a little bit," Will said and stepped back.

Carter's arms felt empty and his body slightly chilled at the loss of contact. What the heck was going on with him? He wasn't crushing on his best friend, he knew that much about himself. But something had definitely shifted in his life lately.

Will made a face. "I hate that I'm not going to be here for Valentine's Day."

Carter pushed his contemplations aside and frowned. "Why? You've got a husband now, your place is with him."

"But we always spent it together," Will said. "It was like the two of us against the rest of the married or committed world."

"Oh, Big Willie, don't you worry about me." Carter gave him a smile he hoped looked genuine. "I've got big plans for Valentine's Day."

Will regarded him closely. "You do?"

"I do. So you don't give me a second thought while you're down in Nashville with that man you swept off his feet out in Boise."

Will grinned. "We met in Williamsville, New York. You know that."

"Oh?" Carter smirked and shrugged. "Anyway. Have no fear, I have an afternoon and evening of debauchery planned that will put the hottest porns to shame."

"Oh? And who will you be porning things up with?" Will asked. "Anyone I know?"

"Oh sweetie, I don't think your phone could handle the Grindr app," Carter said. "I'm afraid it might explode."

"Very funny," Will said. "I mean, are these just random hook ups from Grindr, or someone you've been out with before?"

"It's going to be a chocolate box of sex I'm gifting to myself," Carter said. "Some of the sweets I'm familiar with, and others will be like biting into an unknown treat."

"Be careful," Will said.

"Always, and in all ways," Carter said. "Don't you worry one little iota about me, Big Willie. Since Valentine's Day is this Friday, I'm taking the day off, and will have two days over the weekend to recover."

"Well, I'm going to check in on you from time to time," Will said, "just to make sure you're okay."

"Okay, but if I'm in the middle of a three-way, do you want me to answer your FaceTime call?"

"Uh, no. Thank you." Will shook his head, but with a smile. "I'm going to miss you."

"Me, too," Carter said. "Now, get yourself packed up and safe travels, my beary best friend. Don't spare a thought for me. I'm going to be busier than a beaver in a lumber mill."

CHAPTER TWO

Carter read through the final paragraph of his document one last time and, with a satisfied nod, saved it to the corporate share drive. He read over his list of tasks, and crossed off the last item. Despite what had seemed like an insurmountable number of things to do before his Friday off, he'd actually managed to get everything completed.

"Employee of the month, watch your back," Carter said to himself. "I'm coming to steal your crown."

"You know we don't have employee of the month here, right?"

Carter started and gently glared at Alicia Bakshi, who worked at the neighboring desk. "What are you still doing here?"

"I had a few things to finish up as well," Alicia said. "You were so involved in that gothic novel you've been working on, you didn't even notice me here."

"It's not a gothic novel," Carter said with a sniff. "It might lean a bit toward the horror genre, but it's definitely not gothic. Anyway, I would have thought you'd be out of here right at five to get the kids."

"My husband's picking them up and taking them to a movie

tonight," Alicia said. "That's his Valentine's Day gift to me. I get an evening on my own."

"And you're spending that time here at the office?" Carter shook his head. "You're crazy."

She chuckled. "That is very possible. I think I've managed three consecutive hours of sleep each night the past two weeks."

"I take it that sleep wasn't interrupted for fun times with Santosh?"

"Far and away from fun times with my husband," Alicia said with a tired sigh. "If it's not one kid up puking, then another has a nightmare or a project due, or I have work I need to get done. It's been a tough couple of weeks."

Carter made a face. "Sorry to hear that. But you should really get the hell out of here and enjoy some peace and quiet."

"Yeah, I'm about ready to leave. Since I had the time today, I wanted to finish up a few things. Did I hear you say earlier you're taking tomorrow off?"

"I am. I'm giving myself a three-day weekend of Valentine's fun."

"Ah, Valentine's Day," Alicia said with a sigh. "It used to be so much fun."

"You're getting an evening to yourself tonight," Carter said. "That's going to be nice, isn't it?"

"Yeah, it's nice," Alicia said. "But it's not like back when I was single. A bunch of girlfriends and I would all get together and go out to the bars. Oh my God, we had so much fun. Met a lot of handsome guys, went on some follow up dates. It was a good time. I miss those girls."

"Hitting the bar with friends is the best," Carter said, and felt a pang of loneliness at the thought of Will out of town for this Valentine's Day.

"What are your plans?" Alicia asked.

Carter assessed her, taking in the bruised and puffy skin

beneath her tired, hooded eyes and the dreamy expression coupled with a mischievous grin. He couldn't tell her he was going to wallow in hedonist entertainment, so he came up with something.

"I'm going to hit a few bars and see where my luck takes me."

"With a group of friends?"

Carter managed a smile as he nodded and thought again about Will being so far away. "Yeah, a little group of us will be going out."

"That sounds so fun." Alicia sighed, then sat bolt upright and widened her eyes. "Oh my God! You should do the Cupid Crawl!"

"I'm sorry, the what now?"

"The Cupid Crawl!" Alicia sat at her desk and started clicking her mouse and typing on her keyboard. "I'm still on the mailing list, and they just sent out an updated list of bars. It's a bar crawl that hits a bunch of bars on Valentine's Day. My friends and I did it a couple of times, and Santosh and I even went on it when we first started dating."

"You know, as fun as bar hopping with a bunch of drunk straight people sounds, it's not really what I had in mind."

"No, no, it's not just straight bars," Alicia said, still focused on her computer. "That's the best part. It's a mix of gay and straight. It's really a lot of fun. And no one ever gets out of control. I can't remember the name of the guy who organizes it, but it's a fun event. Here it is. I'm sending it to your work email."

Carter's laptop pinged with a new message alert, but he couldn't look away when Alicia turned her attention back to him. Her face glowed and her expression was practically pleading with him to go on this damn bar crawl, most likely so she could live vicariously through his experience.

"Well, it sounds interesting— "

"Please go on the Cupid Crawl," Alicia said. "Please. Go have a fun and crazy night out for me and my girls. All of us are married with kids now, so we don't go on these kinds of events any longer. Hell, we don't even get together to have a glass of wine any more. I miss those girls." She sighed, then looked back at him. "It would make me feel so good tomorrow to know you were having as much fun as I used to."

"I'll think about it, how's that?" Carter offered.

"I really think you'd enjoy it," she said. "There were some hot guys there. And they dressed up like Cupid, with feathered wings and little loin cloths. Lots of hotness on display."

Carter gave her a dubious look. "Was it only hot guys dressed that way?"

"Well, a lot of the girls wore cute Cupid outfits too, is that what you mean?"

"No, I mean, were all the guys dressed as Cupid able to pull off the costume?"

"Oh." Alicia shrugged and looked away. "Well, no, not all of them." She turned back quick and pointed at him. "But the majority of them looked great. A majority!"

"Yeah, okay."

"You will not be disappointed."

Carter chuckled and turned back to his laptop. "You know disappointment is my default setting."

"That's why I'm suggesting you go on this bar crawl."

He looked over to find her staring at him with puppy dog eyes. With a shake of his head and a dramatic sigh, he opened the email she'd sent and clicked on Print. The printer down the hall kicked into life, and Carter heard it roll out a sheet of paper.

"Okay, I've printed out your email," Carter said. "But no promises!"

Alicia smiled and stared off into the distance with a longing expression. "I had such good times on the Cupid Crawl."

"As compared to all the joy you've experienced being married and having kids?" Carter asked.

She blinked and the longing turned into surprise and, maybe, a touch of guilt. "No! Oh, no. Nothing compares to marriage and kids. I mean, I had fun on the Cupid Crawl and, yeah, sometimes I miss those simpler days of being single. But Santosh and I have a really great marriage, and three beautiful kids."

"And they're all out of your house right now, but you're here trying to talk me into going on a bar crawl tomorrow," Carter said. He jerked a thumb over his shoulder in the direction of the exit. "Get your ass out of that chair and get home and soak in a tub and drink several glasses of wine and listen to John Mayer on repeat."

Alicia laughed, then leaned on the edge of her desk and lowered her voice. "How did you know I like John Mayer?"

"I've seen your Spotify playlist on your screen," Carter said. "John Mayer is in heavy rotation."

"He is a dream. And what a songwriter."

"And you're wasting time here that you could be spending listening to him while you soak in a tub."

"You're right. I'm out of here."

Carter watched her quickly pack her stuff into three bags she carried in and out every day. He had no idea what all those bags contained, but at different times during the workday, Carter would catch her digging into one or all three for something. Alicia pulled a knit cap on her head and slung one bag over each shoulder before picking up the third and smiling at him.

"Go on the crawl."

"Go soak in a tub," Carter replied.

"You'll have fun," Alicia said as she tromped down the aisle in her snow boots.

"Enjoy your alone time," Carter called after her.

"Go on the Cupid Crawl!" Alicia shouted back before she rounded the corner to the elevators.

Carter heard the distant ding of the elevator arriving, the rasp of the doors sliding open then closed, and then the floor was silent. He focused on his laptop again, writing up two more emails and sending them off before he closed the program and shut his computer down. Standing up, he pulled on his coat and hat, stuffed his laptop in his messenger bag, then pushed in his chair. His three day weekend awaited, and he was looking forward to lots of sexy shenanigans for Valentine's Day tomorrow.

He pulled on his gloves and headed for the elevators. Once he'd pressed the elevator call button, he remembered the printout of Alicia's email, and made a face as he looked back down the hall. Did he really think he'd want to go on a bar crawl with a mixed bag of people he didn't know?

"Ugh, if I don't have it with me, I'm going to want it."

He returned to the printer and grabbed the paper off the tray. As he stuffed it in the outer pocket of his messenger bag, the elevator dinged to announce its arrival, and he hurried to catch it before the doors shut. Maybe the Cupid Crawl in combination with his Grindr app would be fun. He might find a host of hot gay or bi guys looking to party, or even a straight guy who was curious to see why all his buddies have been raving about mutual masturbation.

CHAPTER THREE

Friday morning, even though he had the day off, Carter awoke early. He showered, shaved, and searched through his closet for something to wear. The Cupid Crawl was in the back of his mind, behind a sampler of whatever Grindr had to offer. He selected a burgundy button down shirt and black chinos and laid them across the back of the easy chair in the corner of his bedroom. Still in his bathrobe, he stretched out across his bed and opened the Grindr app.

"Slim pickings this morning," Carter mumbled as he scrolled through the profiles. "Where's MeatMan1969 and BiggerThanUXXX69? I thought for sure they'd be online."

Carter didn't see a profile that caught his interest, so he got up and slipped his phone into the pocket of his bathrobe. He busied himself making a light breakfast and brewing a pot of coffee while watching the local morning news. There was a spot about the Cupid Crawl, and Carter paused the program until he could grab his egg white omelet with fruit and a large mug of coffee. He pressed Play and watched the female reporter interview a few people about the Cupid Crawl. A dozen handsome and scantily dressed men wandered past in the background, and Carter sat up straighter.

"Hello," he said. "Looks like there might be several sweets available at this all day drunk fest. Hmm."

The reporter pulled a man into frame who wore a Hawaiian-style shirt and gave the camera a huge smile. Speaking to the camera, the reporter said, "This is Vic Panella, the organizer of the Cupid Crawl." She turned to Vic and asked, "So are there spots still available for people interested in joining the Cupid Crawl today?"

"There are some spots available," Vic said. "But people need to get down here quick if they're interested, because we have a limited number of seats on the shuttles."

"There you have it folks," the reporter said as she looked into the camera. "If you're looking to have some fun today, come down to That Corner Bar and sign up for the Cupid Crawl. It looks like it's going to be quite a fun time." She half-turned to the crowd that had formed behind her—a mix of men and women, some dressed as Cupids, others as angels, and still others wearing a lot of red—and said, "You going to have fun today, guys?"

The group cheered, and the reporter laughed before handing things off to the anchors back in the studio.

Carter pulled his phone from the pocket of his robe and checked out Grindr again. Still no one he wanted to connect with. Well, that settled it. Looked like he was going on the Cupid Crawl after all.

∽

WHEN CARTER STEPPED from the Lyft car, he blinked in surprise at the crowd spilling out the door of That Corner Bar. He sometimes went to the bars on his own, but today felt different. He attributed it to the pressure of it being Valentine's Day, and a big date day. But still, he felt a bit nervous. The crowd had already been drinking and he could hear boisterous laughter out here on the street. Getting through the crowd at the door and inside to find the organizer seemed a very daunting task, and Carter decided to walk up and down the block to work up his nerve. He turned away from the door of That Corner Bar and stepped right into someone.

"Oh, shit, I'm sorry," Carter said.

"No worries," the man said. "You already sign up?"

"No, but, you know, it's all right. I think I've changed my mind."

"You sure? Lots of people in there waiting to meet you," the man said.

Carter took a step back and gave him a once over. This was the man the reporter had interviewed at the end of her piece, Vic the organizer. Carter could now see that Vic's Hawaiian-style shirt was covered with hearts and arrows and winged cherubs. The black framed glasses Vic wore held thick lenses and the variety of neon signs in the windows of That Corner Bar gleamed across the top of his shaved head.

"Have they been asking for me by name?" Carter said as he crossed his arms.

Vic smirked. "Only one way to find out." He held up a clipboard with a sign up sheet. "Just a few spots left. This could be your lucky day. Cupid's been slinging his arrows right and left already."

"Sounds pretty dangerous," Carter said. "You've got insurance, right?"

He grinned. "Nope. But I can guarantee you'll meet at least three interesting people today."

"Only three?"

"At least three."

Carter looked at the crowded doorway again. He *did* want to do something other than scroll through Grindr and wait in his apartment for someone who may or may not arrive. He'd feel more confident if Will were with him, but it was probably time he got used to doing things on his own. And, besides, if he really hated it, he could always duck out early and grab a Lyft back home.

"All right, you convinced me."

Carter took the clipboard and wrote his name. Vic pointed out the charge, which Carter thought was a very reasonable amount, so he handed over his credit card. After Vic swiped it through a reader on his phone, he handed the card back and held his phone out so Carter could sign his name with his finger.

"You will not be sorry Carter Walsh," the man said, then extended his hand, which Carter shook. "My name's Vic Panella. I've organized the Cupid Crawl for the last ten years."

"Well, that's longer than I've been old enough to drink," Carter said with a coquettish smile.

Vic grinned. "You're going fit in well with this crowd." He bowed and waved Carter toward the crowded bar doorway. "Make the most of this day of love."

"Before I get all up in that mass of angel wings and body spray, when do we hit the gay bars?"

"You're a planner, I see," Vic said. "I like that. We start here, and everyone gets to know each other for a couple of hours. After that, we board shuttles and head to Intentions."

"You're hitting a gay bar on your second stop?" Carter raised his eyebrows. "That's nicely diverse of you."

"I aim to please," Vic said. "Two to three hours there, depending on how everyone's feeling. After that, the third bar is Hip Check."

"That's a sports bar, isn't it?"

"Again, I aim to please everyone," Vic said. "And Hip Check has a large beer selection along with a big dance floor."

"There's a dance floor in a sports bar?"

"Hey, sports lovers like to dance, too."

Carter shrugged. "I guess."

"Hommes is next."

"That's a fun gay bar," Carter said. "Nice French theme decor. You've done your homework."

"Oh, I've been around," Vic said with a wink. "After that we hit Minor Chords, the dueling piano bar, for some drunken sing-alongs, and then finish up at Cheeky Monkey."

"You're finishing up the day of drinking and scantily clad men and women at the gay and lesbian mecca of Cheeky Monkey?"

"Everyone who signs up for the Cupid Crawl knows the bars and schedule. If anyone's uncomfortable with it, they're free to duck out early." Vic crossed his arms. "Does the schedule pass inspection?"

"Yeah, of course," Carter said. "I just wanted to make sure you had it all covered, you know. Like you didn't need some suggestions from a seasoned barfly like myself."

Vic stepped closer and put a big hand on Carter's shoulder. He smiled and said in a gentle voice, "I won't let anything happen to you, Carter. I'm in charge of all this chaos, and all you need to do is relax and enjoy yourself."

Carter nodded as a whisper of relief went through him. "I can see you know what you're doing, Vic. So I guess I'll go in and meet some new friends."

"Let's go in together," Vic said. "I need to check on a few things."

Vic led the way, squeezing past the men and women standing in the doorway and forging a path for Carter to follow. At first, Carter thought he was way overdressed. The men he slid past were shirtless, some wearing just white loin cloths or even cloth diapers along with feathered wings strapped around their broad chests. These men gave him a brief glance, maybe a quick smile, but were busy talking to each other or women who were also baring a lot of skin. Didn't these people realize it was February in Boston?

When he reached the bar, Carter was relieved to see people wearing shirts and pants instead of just diapers and short shorts. Vic leaned in over the bar and said to the bartender, "Don, this is my good friend, Carter. Put his first two drinks on my tab."

"Oh, you don't have to do that," Carter insisted. "I have money."

"Happy Valentine's Day, Carter," Vic said. "The first two drinks are on me to help you relax. I'm going to make a round of the bar, but when I return, I hope to find you talking with someone, and not just leaning on the bar all alone."

"I know how to socialize," Carter said.

"Oh, I'm sure you do."

Vic winked again before threading his way through the crowd, greeting people as he slid past them. Carter ordered a beer from Don, and then fished a couple of singles out of his wallet for a tip. He lifted his bottle to salute Don and had just taken a swig when a piercingly high voice shrieked from just behind him. The sound startled him so much he choked on his beer and started to cough. He turned, coughing and sputtering, and squinted through his tears at the woman standing behind him.

Auburn hair done up tall, bright green eyes that could be nothing other than colored contact lenses, a pert, upturned nose, and a broad mouth filled with teeth laser-whitened to solar flare level.

Carter's heart stuttered with surprise and dread as he struggled to clear his airway.

"I saw you walk in and had to come over and see if it was really you!" she exclaimed.

With a final clearing of his throat, Carter managed a smile and said, "Lizzie. Hello! What a treat to see you."

Lizzie's smile widened even further and she crossed her arms.

It was then Carter noticed she wore what looked like a sports bra with a pair of white wings strapped to her shoulders, and a sheer white shift around her waist that showed off a pair of black panties trimmed with lace.

"As I live and breathe," Lizzie said with a shake of her head. "Carter the Farter."

CHAPTER FOUR

Carter winced. He had worked with Lizzie—or, rather, Dizzy Frizzy Lizzie, as he and Will called her—a few years ago at a previous employer. During one hellacious week of days packed with meetings that lasted nearly all day, and included lunch which consisted of fast-delivery sandwiches, followed by late nights to catch up on the work set aside to attend the meetings, Carter had finally found himself at his desk one evening. He'd thought he'd been alone, and released a tiny bit of gas he'd been holding in for awhile, surprising himself with the squeaking noise of the fart. Lizzie had, of course, arrived in time to hear it, and bestowed on him the nickname Carter the Farter.

Because apparently, they had been project managers in second grade.

And now here she was once again, Dizzy Frizzy Lizzie, and some of the first words out of her mouth had to be that fucking childish nickname.

Carter hated it. But, more importantly, he hated that it got to him so much.

"Hello Lizzie," Carter said with a grim smile as he looked her up and down. "I see you kept that casual Friday outfit you were so fond of."

Lizzie laughed again and put a hand on his shoulder. "Oh, CF, I do miss working with you."

"I'm sure you do," Carter said, then noticed a man looming behind Lizzie's right shoulder. "You've got a lurker."

"What?" Lizzie turned. "Oh! That's not a lurker. That's Harry."

Carter checked Harry out a little closer. He was big, six foot four at least, with dark hair and a wide face that tapered to a square jaw with a deep dimple. He wore black plastic-framed glasses and sported a mustache long enough to allow him to wax the ends so they stuck out a bit past his lips.

Harry was apparently trying to bring back 1970's porn star chic. Or imitate a villain from a silent movie.

There was so much going on with Lizzie's lurker friend, the only thought that really stood out in Carter's mind was Harry was a whole lot of man.

"Hi there," Harry said with a flash of a smile and a quick wave.

"Hi. Nice..." Carter stopped, a bit at a loss for what to say next. He finally settled on, "Glasses."

"Oh, thanks." Harry adjusted the frames and looked off toward the bar, sliding his gaze back to Carter before quickly shifting it away again.

"Are you two dating?" Carter asked Lizzie.

"Harry?" Lizzie laughed. "And me?" Her laugh intensified in volume and duration, then she looked at Harry. "Would you date me?"

Harry shifted nervously and flicked his gaze between Carter and Lizzie. He was probably sensing some kind of trap, and rightly so, based on Carter's experience with Dizzy Frizzy Lizzie.

Finally, Harry gave a simple shrug. "Probably not a good idea, since we work together."

Lizzie laughed again and slapped a hand flat on Harry's chest, pulling Carter's attention to how he was dressed. Harry wore a white T-shirt with a graphic of cartoon abs stretched tight across his chest and the slight swell of his belly. A pair of stone washed jeans hugged big thighs and, from what Carter could see, a well-rounded ass. New Balance sneakers completed his ensemble, which apparently was 'urban hipster tech geek'.

"You are a riot!" Lizzie nearly shouted, then suddenly turned back to Carter with a sly look. "Are you hitting on my VD escort?"

"VD?" Carter said a little louder than intended, and several guys turned to look with slightly alarmed expressions.

"Yeah, CF, VD," Lizzie said. "Valentine's Day, silly. Harry's my VD escort today, and I want to know if you've set your sights on him."

"Oh my God, you cannot keep calling him that," Carter said.

"Thank you," Harry muttered and blew out a heavy breath.

Carter continued without acknowledging him. "And, no, I'm one hundred percent for sure not hitting on him." He heard how his statement sounded and made a face as he met Harry's gaze. "Sorry, I didn't mean that the way it sounded."

Beneath the mustache—it was so distracting!—Carter saw Harry's lips press tight together.

"No worries," Harry said. "You're a little too fancy for my taste."

Carter raised his eyebrows. "Fancy?"

A couple of hot guys brushed past them, heading to the bar, and Lizzie set off in pursuit without saying a word. Carter stared up at Harry who stared right back.

"Fancy?" Carter repeated.

Harry waved a hand up and down between them. "Well, look at you."

Carter blinked. "Are you saying I'm acting like a fancy boy just by standing here?"

Harry frowned and cocked his head. "Fancy boy?" Realization hit and his eyes widened and his mouth dropped open. "No! I didn't mean fancy like... like that. No. Not like that at all. I meant fancy as in you're dressed fancy for a bar crawl."

Carter took a long drink from his beer as he considered Harry. The man looked as if he genuinely meant what he said, but Carter didn't want to let him off that easily. Any friend of Lizzie's would ultimately be trouble, he had no doubt about that.

"Just because I put some care and thought into my choice of wardrobe today, as compared to your ensemble, which looks like you grabbed it off the rack from a John Hughes movie, doesn't make me fancy. It means I have self-respect."

"I—"

"Nice to meet you, Harry," Carter said, and lifted his beer bottle in acknowledgement. "Enjoy the crawl."

He moved off into the crowd without giving Harry a chance to respond. Any good feeling Carter had managed to muster up about the Cupid Crawl had been deflated by Dizzy Frizzy Lizzie and her Lurch-sized shadow with the Chia Pet mustache. Lizzie's presence through the entire event would not only feel like running a cheese grater across his brain, but she would most likely hamper any chance he might have of meeting a guy. He could already imagine her sauntering up and taking over any conversation he'd be having, and most likely calling him Carter the Farter in front of every guy who showed even a passing interest in him. He'd farted one time. One time! She really needed to let that go.

With these recent developments, it might be time for him to bail on the Cupid Crawl. He could grab a Lyft back to his apartment, change into something completely slutty, and scroll through Grindr for a hookup or five. And if that didn't pan out, he'd put on sweats and watch some ridiculous romantic comedies.

THE CUPID CRAWL

He was in charge of his own happiness for Valentine's Day, and he wasn't about to let some big mouth from his past take that away.

After chugging the last of his beer, he set the empty on the bar and turned toward the exit. His phone buzzed and he pulled it from his pocket. A FaceTime request from Will. He debated ignoring the call, then decided he could stand to see a friendly face right then. Besides, Will might need some coaching about his big event. With a moment to gather his resolve and put on a chipper face, he accepted the call and headed for the door to the street.

Will's face filled the screen, making Carter feel simultaneously better and more lonely. How weird was that?

"Hey there," Carter said. "It's loud in here, give me a minute."

Will frowned and held the phone closer as if inspecting Carter's whereabouts. Carter could just make out his question: "Where are you?"

"I'm at a bar," Carter shouted back. "Hold on, I'm going outside to be able to talk."

Carter had to slide between a half dozen shirtless men wearing wings strapped to their shoulders, and he saw Will's eyebrows go up.

"Hey there." One of the men flashed a dazzling smile, then leaned in closer to peer at Carter's phone. "Is that your boyfriend?"

"No, just a friend," Carter said, and returned a smile of his own. "I haven't been struck by Cupid's arrow yet."

The man—sexy with a blond buzz cut and a patch of fine blond hair between his firm, square pecs—pulled a small suction-cup-tipped arrow from a fanny pack covered with red sequins. The man licked the suction cup, and then pressed it to Carter's forehead.

"Now you have," he said.

"Smooth," Carter said.

He stepped outside and gasped at the sudden bite of cold air. Returning his attention to his phone, he mustered up a smile and said, "Hi, Big Willie."

"Where are you and what is that thing stuck to your forehead?" Will asked.

"Oh, it's a long story." Carter pulled the arrow free with a quiet *pop* of releasing suction, then rubbed at his forehead. "Did it leave a mark?"

"Looks like someone gave you a hickey on your forehead."

"Damn." Carter rubbed harder. "How about now?"

"Now your whole forehead is red, like you have a rash or poison ivy or something."

Carter sighed and gave up, tucking the arrow into his back pocket. "Maybe the cold air will help. So, how are you? How are things out in Oklahoma?"

"I'm in Nashville," Will said. "And things are fine. The event doesn't start until late afternoon, so Rex and I went down to the hotel pool for a swim."

A man peered over Will's shoulder and waved. "Hi, Carter!"

Rex Garland, Will's husband of six weeks, was model hot with a big heart and down home manners. His dark hair was still damp from the pool, and his scruffy beard made him look even more sexy.

"Hi, Rex," Carter said. "Congrats on the nomination. I hope you win and you both have fun tonight."

Rex moved in closer over Will's shoulder and said, "I'm already a winner." He kissed Will on the cheek, waved to Carter, then stepped out of view.

Will's face practically glowed from the heat of his blush, and Carter would not have been surprised if Will spontaneously erupted into an orgasm. Managing to push down an envious sigh,

Carter said, "Well, I'd say your trip to Nashville is off to a titillating start."

"Yeah, it's been pretty great." Will's smile was so broad and bright he looked like a toothpaste commercial. "So how and where are you?"

"Well, one, I'm fine, thank you. And, two, I let a co-worker talk me into attending this bar crawl some guy organized called the Cupid Crawl."

"Is it a gay bar crawl?" Will asked.

"It's a mix of straight and gay," Carter said. "I'm at the first one right now, at a bar called That Corner Bar. It's pretty crowded already and people are still arriving."

"Oh, interesting. So no rotating Grindr dates?" Will said. "You're actually out in public talking to people?"

"For now." Carter glanced back at the door to find the hot guy who'd stuck the arrow on his forehead casually watching him. Maybe the Cupid Crawl wouldn't be so bad after all. If he could manage to avoid Lizzie and Harry.

"What do you mean 'for now'?" Will asked. "You thinking of ducking out early?"

"Possibly. Like a bad soap opera, a figure from my past has shown up."

"Uh-oh, an ex?" Will's eyes widened. "It's not Phillip, is it? Oh hell, I hope it's not him."

"Relax, it's not Phillip." Carter smiled in the direction of the hot arrow-sticker cupid. "It's kind of worse, in a way."

Will frowned. "Who could be worse than the guy who cheated on you and stole a bunch of money from your bank account?"

"Lizzie Foster."

Will's mouth dropped open. "Dizzy Frizzy Lizzie from Preston-Wellis?"

"One and the same."

"Oh shit! Does her hair still look like a nightmare mated with a lot of humidity?"

"Not really," Carter said with a chuckle. "She must have found an industrial strength hair straightener or something."

"I see." Will chewed his lower lip a moment. "Didn't she give you an, um, unfortunate nickname?"

"Carter the Farter?" He nodded. "Yes, she did. And that's how she greeted me. At top Lizzie volume."

"Oh no."

"Oh yes. And then she introduced me to this really tall, odd guy with a mustache right out of straight porn who looked me over and called me 'fancy'."

"Fancy? Like a slur for being gay?"

"Well, that's how I took it, at first. But then he tried to say it was because of how I was dressed, but I'm not sure I believe him."

Will frowned. "Hold the phone out, let me see what you're wearing."

Carter smirked. "What are *you* wearing?"

"Just show me your outfit."

"You're no fun," Carter said with a pout, but held the phone at arm's length and lifted his chin. "Well? How do I look?"

Will shrugged. "You look fancy."

"You are no help." Carter brought the phone close again. "Anyway, enough about me. How are you? All ready for the award ceremony later today?"

Will glanced off to the side, probably making sure Rex wasn't nearby, then held the phone closer and lowered his voice. "I'm pretty nervous."

"Hey, you've got this. I mean it. Rex is so head over heels in love with you it's ridiculous, and you're going to look fabulous in that outfit."

"Thanks to you," Will said. "You really have a good eye for fashion, which is why you look fancy."

THE CUPID CRAWL

"All right, I get it."

Carter shook his head and glanced back at the doorway. The arrow-sticker was talking and laughing with a couple of other hot guys. Maybe he should continue with the Cupid Crawl for another bar two, and see if anything more developed with the sexy arrow-sticker or one of the other hotties.

"So are you going to stick it out?" Will asked.

"In official terms, that's referred to as indecent exposure."

Will smirked. "What am I going to do with you?"

"Love me from afar?"

"Always."

"Yeah, I'll probably give the Cupid Crawl one more bar to make a good impression before I bail. The organizer told me we're going to hit Intentions next."

"Oh yeah? You like that place. Sounds like it will be a fun day."

"Here's hoping." Carter held up his free hand to show he had crossed his fingers. "Good luck today, Big Willie. Call me if you need some rah-rah mojo."

"Right back at ya, Cartier."

"Go get 'em, Carter!" Rex shouted from offscreen, and Carter and Will both laughed.

"Tell that big lug I expect him to write a song about me someday soon," Carter said. "Something sassy, sexy, and upbeat. No minor keys."

"I'll relay your demands," Will said with a grin.

"See that you do." Carter smiled. "Have a good time, Big Willie."

"You too," Will said. "And Carter?"

"Yeah?"

"Happy Valentine's Day," Will said, and the depth of sincere affection in his expression caused tears to prickle at the corners of Carter's eyes. "I love you."

"Love you right back," Carter said. "Now have fun and frolic."

"You, too."

Carter disconnected the call and shivered in another gust of wind. He hadn't wanted to bother with a coat when moving from bar to bar, and now the cold cut right through his shirt—correction, his *fancy* shirt.

Crossing his arms tight over his chest, Carter walked back to the door. He slowly sidled between the men and women lingering there until he stood face-to-face with the handsome arrow-sticker.

"Hello again," the man said.

"Oh, hi," Carter said, acting casual.

"How's your friend?"

"He's fine," Carter said. "We usually spend Valentine's Day together, so he wanted to check in."

"Friends with benefits?" the man asked with a grin.

"We dated for a couple of weeks before realizing we'd be better off as friends," Carter said.

The man looked impressed. "Not many people can make that work."

"We're not many people." Carter extended his hand. "I'm Carter."

"Frank." His grip was strong, and his smile killer.

"Carter the Farter, there you are!"

Carter's smile evaporated the same time Frank's eyebrows went up and his mouth dropped open in surprise and amusement.

Yep, it was going to be a very long crawl.

CHAPTER FIVE

Frank choked back a laugh and released Carter's hand. His gaze shifted to a spot just over Carter's shoulder.

"Friend of yours?" Frank asked, fighting to keep his grin in check, but losing the battle in spectacular fashion.

"Fiend, maybe," Carter said. "Not friend. Just ignore her."

"Um, she's kind of tough to ignore. Especially with her lurker."

Carter turned in the narrow and crowded entryway to find Lizzie standing directly behind him. Hovering over her shoulder like some kind of giant, five-steps-out-of-fashion bodyguard was Harry, stroking his mustache.

"Lizzie—" Carter started.

"Farter," Lizzie interrupted with a smirk.

Carter looked over his shoulder at Frank, and flashed a smile he hoped looked normal and not as close to the brink of madness as he felt. "Would you excuse me for a tick?"

"Okay." Frank appeared uneasy, and Carter assumed he could sense the growing tension.

"Thanks so much." Carter turned back to Lizzie and gestured toward the interior of the bar. "Let's have a chat, shall we?"

"I've really missed our chats," Lizzie said.

Instead of turning away and entering the bar, Lizzie leaned in close and extended her arm over Carter's shoulder. Her attention was directed behind him, and she'd fixed her face into an expression Carter could only assume was meant to be smoldering, but in reality seemed more in line with gastric bloating.

"Lizzie Foster," she said. "Open to any and all experiences."

From behind him, Carter heard Frank say, "Um, hi. I'm Frank." And from the man's tone, he wasn't quite that open to any experiences with Lizzie, and, by extension, most likely Carter himself. She stood so close to Carter the sweet and flowery scent of her perfume filled his nose and throat. He tried to step back, but people had crowded in the doorway, trapping him in place. A sick feeling of claustrophobia clawed at the edges of his temper. He needed to get some space quick, but Lizzie was practically pressed against him as she "flirted" with Frank.

Carter held his arms out and tried to find a spot on Lizzie to place his hands that wouldn't set her off. Hips and waist seemed too intimate, especially since she only wore a pair of black panties beneath the sheer white shift. His hands hovered in the space around her body as he tried to decide where to place them and push her back. No matter what he decided, he knew it would come back to bite him.

Before he made the difficult decision, however, Lizzie took a couple steps back. Carter drew in a deep breath, then slipped past her and into a pocket of space between groups of people. Turning, Carter found Harry watching him, one of his big hands gently gripping Lizzie's free hand. Carter realized Harry had taken her hand and drawn her back far enough for him to escape.

He gave Harry a nod of thanks, and remained where he was,

about ten feet away from them. Harry nodded back just before Lizzie pulled her hand free and slapped him on the chest.

"Harry, you sly dog," Lizzie said. "Are you trying to make out with me?"

"Um, no," Harry said. "We're co-workers, remember?"

"Secret office affairs are the best though," Lizzie said, then looked at Carter. "There you are! How'd you move so fast? Oh, do the farts give you super speed?"

Before Carter could open his mouth, Harry tugged Lizzie in closer and whispered something to her. Carter watched Lizzie's expression shift from outgoing party girl to something almost wounded.

"Oh, Carter!" Lizzie exclaimed. "I didn't know my Farter nickname was so upsetting to you."

"Oh my God," Carter muttered, then said louder, "Please stop calling me that!"

"Okay, yeah, sure," Lizzie said, nodding rapidly. "I'll stop. No more Farter, I promise." She clapped a hand over her mouth, and her eyes widened as people standing nearby looked between them with a mixture of amused and disgusted expressions.

"Please, stop," Carter said. "You guys stay there." He held up both hands palms out in a "stop" gesture. "And I'll go find somewhere else to... be. Okay?"

"What?" Lizzie practically shouted.

Carter waved and turned away to lose himself in the crowd. What the actual hell was that about? Lizzie had always been a handful at work, but drunk Lizzie was fifteen times worse! He was really glad he'd never made a habit of going to happy hour outings with the team at his previous job.

He made a wide circuit of the bar, smiling at the men and trying to pick out candidates who might be open to a potential hook-up. Some of the men were incredibly hot, but Carter was surprised by a shift in his assessment of them. Sure, he looked at physical features, but something seemed to have shifted in his brain, because now he caught himself evaluating their boyfriend potential, a frustratingly difficult to evaluate quality. He wondered how considerate the guy was to his partner. How well he communicated. What his favorite pastimes were. What side of the bed he preferred.

Good God, it was like Carter's brain was husband shopping while his dick was only interested in a quickie. And how the hell would he be able to tell a man's potential to be a good boyfriend anyway? Was it something about his eyes? Or maybe his smile? Or maybe the way he carried himself?

Carter reached the opposite end of the bar from where he'd left Lizzie and Harry, and got in line behind a large group, a good mix of men and women, all dressed in red and pink. As he waited for the group to order and pay for their drinks, Carter checked his Grindr app. A number of profiles were listed close by—one as close as six feet, which Carter assumed was a member of the group ahead of him. He read each profile and checked out the guys around him to try and make a match.

A tall, handsome man with dark hair and a nice scruff of beard was watching him with a knowing smile. When he caught Carter's eye, the man held up his phone before looking down and typing something on it. A moment later, the man lifted his gaze and nodded to the phone in Carter's hand. Carter found a message waiting on his Grindr app, from the profile VersatileJoe75, which read, *Nice shirt. I hope it didn't cost a lot, because I'd like to rip it off you.*

Carter smirked and wrote back: *I'm not a bargain fashion shopper. I hope you brought a nice wad of cash.*

VersatileJoe75 smiled when he read Carter's message, and wrote back: *I always pack a nice, big wad. Wanna see?*

Carter did, in fact, want to see, so he tipped his head toward the back hallway which led to the restrooms. VersatileJoe75 grinned and nodded before leaning in to say something to the three men he stood with. Carter stepped out of line—that damn talkative group still hadn't finished getting their drinks, what the hell?—and made his way to the restroom.

There was a line just inside the door, and Carter made a face as he stood behind a man wearing what had to be a full bottle of body spray. Now that he thought about it, a bathroom quickie might not be the best idea during the Cupid Crawl due to the mixed crowd. He really didn't want to get bashed in a bar bathroom. Maybe today would be just for getting to know a guy and deciding to go out later.

The door behind him opened and VersatileJoe75 stepped inside. He stood close behind Carter, close enough to press his bulge against Carter's left ass cheek.

"Crowded in here," Carter said over his shoulder as he fought back a blush.

"I can fix that," VersatileJoe75 whispered. He spoke up and said, "They just announced last call before we get on the shuttle for the next bar."

"Oh shit," a few of the men said.

Those already at the urinals quickly finished up and exited the bathroom, some washing their hands and some not bothering. Carter tried to make a mental list of the men who hadn't washed up, but was too distracted by Joe's proximity.

In a couple of minutes, the bathroom had emptied out. Joe put his hands on Carter's shoulders and walked him toward the larger handicap stall against the far wall. Carter felt the solid line of Joe's erection against his ass, and his own cock responded.

Once inside the stall, Carter turned to say something, but Joe stopped his words with a tongue-heavy kiss, his scruff deliciously scratching across Carter's chin. As they kissed, Carter squeezed Joe's erection through his jeans, earning a quiet moan that sent vibrations into his own mouth.

Joe pulled back and gave him a sexy smirk. "I think my dick needs some air."

"I think my tongue needs some dick," Carter said, and sat on the toilet seat. He unzipped Joe's pants and carefully peeled his briefs down to free his cock.

It was lovely, long and pale, with a broad head that gleamed with a coating of pre-cum. Carter ran his tongue up the length, then took Joe deep into his throat.

"Oh, fucking hell," Joe said with a sigh.

Carter pulled back and looked up, slowly stroking Joe's dick. "You might want to muzzle yourself a bit."

"Oh, kinky," Joe said, then braced himself on the side walls of the stall and nodded.

Carter went back to work. He closed his eyes and savored the taste of Joe's skin and pre-cum. Slowly taking Joe deep into his throat, he paused with his nose buried in the soft, neatly trimmed bush at the base before pulling back equally slow. Gradually he increased his speed and wrapped the fingers of one hand around the hard, hot shaft now slick with his spit. Faster and faster he sucked, Joe gasping quietly above him, and the muscles of his thighs tightening.

"Yeah, just like that," Joe whispered. "Just like that. Keep it up. Oh, yeah. I'm close. Really close. Yes!"

Carter sat back and leaned to one side, hand pumping fast and aiming Joe's dick so his cum splattered across the metal wall. Not one drop stained his shirt or pants. This might be a skill he could add to his resume.

"Damn, that was fucking hot," Joe said, panting a bit and eyes glassy with satisfaction.

"I aim to please," Carter said with a smile.

Joe gestured toward the mess on the wall. "You aimed me well, too." He grabbed a wad of toilet paper and cleaned the tip of his dick, then wiped most of the spunk off the wall.

Carter stood up and Joe tossed the wad of paper into the toilet. He tucked himself away and zipped his jeans, then smiled. Just as he was about to say something, the door to the bathroom banged open and a group of men entered, talking and laughing.

"It's crowded in here now," Joe whispered.

"Yeah," Carter agreed, feeling a bit nervous.

"Hey," one of the new arrivals said on the other side of the stall. "Are there two guys in this stall?"

Carter exchanged a wide-eyed look with Joe.

"Raincheck for me to return the favor?" Joe asked.

Carter nodded, and before he could do or say anything else, Joe opened the stall door and slipped away.

Apparently VersatileJoe75 wasn't as versatile as advertised. Carter made sure his shirt was tucked in, tugged down the cuffs of his sleeves, and then opened the stall door.

Harry, Lizzie's lurker co-worker, stood at the sink washing his hands. Carter met Harry's gaze in the mirror. A twist of something—regret? Embarrassment?—tightened Carter's stomach. He kept his expression open and relaxed—he hoped—and nodded to Harry.

"Hi," Carter said as he stepped up to the sink at the opposite end of the mirror.

"Hello." Harry's voice was cool enough he might as well have freon for blood.

Carter felt a bit guilty as he washed his hands and rinsed out his mouth. Harry was toying with his hair when Carter pull paper towel from the dispenser. Carter wanted to ask if he was going to freshen up his mustache ends as well, but decided against it. Instead, he said, "Thank you for pulling Lizzie off me earlier, and allowing me to escape."

"You're welcome," Harry said. He played with his hair a bit before looking at Carter in the mirror. "Looked like you were getting a little freaked out being stuck there."

"Yeah, I get a little claustrophobic when I can't move around very much."

"So I guess that rules out mummification?" Harry said.

A smirk snuck up on Carter. "Um, yeah. I'd have to give that a strong no."

Harry faced him and flashed a bright smile that lifted the ends of his mustache. "I'll make a note of that. You sticking with the crawl or taking off?"

"I thought about leaving, but I've decided to stay for one more bar," Carter said. "How about you? Find any women who've caught your interest?"

"A couple," Harry said. "But a few more men than I'd thought."

Carter raised his eyebrows. "You're bi?"

"Does that surprise you?"

Carter shrugged. "What? No. I just... It's just that..."

Harry crossed his arms, and fixed him with a steady stare. "Yes?"

"Fine." Carter blew out a breath. "I am surprised, I admit it. Your hair and mustache and the T-shirt kind of threw me off."

"Guys who look like me can't be bi?"

"No, I didn't mean it that way..."

"That's pretty much exactly what you said."

"You're taking it out of context," Carter said, cheeks burning and a tiny knot of tension forming in his chest.

Harry moved two steps closer. "Is there something else you'd rather say? I mean, something that won't dig the hole you're already standing in a lot deeper?"

Carter pressed his lips together, then gave a nod and said, "I'm sorry."

Harry smiled, and it lit up his face, making him look quite handsome. And smug, the bastard. "Apology accepted." He faced the mirror again and combed his fingers through his hair some more. "And I keep the center part because it's the best style for my hair. I know it's out of fashion, but my hair naturally parts in the middle and not the side."

"Sorry again," Carter said.

"One apology is plenty," Harry said. He tweaked the ends of his mustache. "My daughters have been trying to get me to shave off my mustache for years, but I like it."

"Daughters?"

"I have two daughters, fifteen and thirteen."

"So you're married?" Carter asked.

"Was," Harry said. "For fifteen years. Divorced for just over a year."

"Sorry."

Harry looked at him in the mirror. "You're doing a lot of apologizing all of a sudden. Did that trick really take the edge off or something?"

Carter snorted a quiet laugh. "Hardly. Left me hanging, thanks to you."

"Guess it's my turn to apologize," Harry said. "I could give you a hand, if you want."

Carter frowned. "I don't think that's a good idea."

"Because of my mustache and center-parted hair?" Harry turned to face him, crossing his arms and leaning his hip against the counter. "Or because I work with Lizzie?"

"Is there an all of the above option in that list?"

Harry nodded once before turning to head for the door. The music grew louder when he opened it, and he smiled over his shoulder.

"Just for the record, I'm pansexual, not bi. Google it."

He stepped out of the bathroom, and the door closed behind him.

CHAPTER SIX

Carter stared at the door, half expecting Harry to return and drop another snarky comment, but he didn't appear. No one else entered the bathroom either, and Carter glared at his reflection. *Google it.* What the fuck did that mean? Like he didn't know the what it meant when someone told him they were pansexual.

Though almost certain he knew what it meant, he did Google it. A pansexual was attracted to people no matter their biological sex, gender, or gender identity. It was the connection with someone and not how they represented themselves.

"Ha, I did know, Harry. Why don't you Google when mustache waxing went out of style?"

He didn't know, however, that there was a pansexual flag, with three horizontal bars: pink, yellow, and blue. But that was beside the point.

So Harry with the center-parted hair and old-movie villain mustache was a divorced pansexual father of two girls. Carter had a feeling the hair and mustache had been high on Harry's ex-wife's list of reasons for divorce.

Unless Harry had been the one to initiate the divorce.

Carter shook his head at his reflection as he slid his phone into his pocket. None of it mattered. Today was about opportunity and indulgence. Since the blowjob with VersatileJoe75—correction, the blowjob he had *given* to VersatileJoe75 and not received—hadn't smoothed down his rough edges, Carter wanted to see if he could find someone who might be able to get him off.

He washed his hands and gave himself a stern look. "You get back on that horse, young man." He paused a moment before saying, "Or get on someone hung like a horse." He smiled and gave himself a wink. "That's the spirit."

As he stepped out of the bathroom, Carter flinched at the sudden whine of feedback through an amplifier. The music that had been thumping along at mid-volume lowered, and then Vic's voice boomed through the sound system.

"Hey there, Cupid Crawlers, you ready for the first giveaway?"

Everyone in the bar cheered, and Carter waded into the crowd until he could see the raised stage at the far end of the dance floor. Vic squinted in the glare of the stage lights shaking, the contents of a large manila envelope.

"Get your tickets out, Crawlers," Vic said. "This is the first of six prize giveaways today. One prize per person."

As Carter pulled his ticket stub from his pocket, feathers stroked across his face. He jerked back in surprise.

A young woman who looked like she wasn't even old enough to drink yet stood close by. She had pale skin, delicate features, and heavy, dark eye makeup. If they had been in the 1990's, Carter would call her Goth, or maybe emo. He was surprised to see she wore a set of large, black-feathered wings, and a long black dress beneath a black velvet jacket. She was dressed more like an angel of Death than a cherub slinging love arrows around. In contrast to her clothing and wings, her long hair was a brilliant shade of platinum blond.

"Sorry. They have a mind of their own," she said, and shifted her shoulders back and forth to make the big wings move. "Like Doctor Octopus in the *Spider-Man* comics, but only they're wings instead of arms."

"Um, sure," he said. "No problem."

She smirked. "You think I'm weird."

"A little, yeah."

"Honest, too. I like that." She turned to face him, and extended her hand, wings nearly knocking over a woman standing nearby. "I'm Ivy."

Carter shook her hand gently, not wanting to press the small bones together too hard. "Carter."

"Nice to meet you," Ivy said. "You here with your boyfriend or a group of friends?"

"What makes you think I'm gay?" Carter asked with a frown.

"Oh, I don't know." Ivy looked him up and down. "You're dressed really... nice?"

He pursed his lips. "Fancy?"

Ivy's face lit up and she pointed at him as she jumped up and down, her wings trembling and weaving. "Yes! Fancy!" She settled and her face shifted quickly into a mixed expression of boredom and loathing. "So, are you here with someone special or a group?"

"Nope. I'm on my own today."

"Yeah? Me, too. Couldn't find anyone who wanted to come out and play with me." She blew a strand of hair out of her eyes. "Not even my parole officer, who at least takes me to Costco."

"You're parole...?" Carter crossed his arms and gave her a look. "That's a joke, right?"

Ivy shrugged, her wings shifting with the movement. "I dunno. Could be."

"Okay, Crawlers," Vic said into the microphone, and Carter and Ivy both turned toward him. "Here comes the first winning number."

Vic held the manila envelope over his head and made a big show of shaking it vigorously. Carter gripped his ticket stub tight and wondered what the prize would be. Maybe a couple's massage? What the hell would he do with that if he won? Give it to Will and Rex? Maybe a romantic getaway to a swanky hotel? He liked staying in hotels sometimes, so he'd keep that one for himself. Maybe order up some Grindr appetizers and dessert between having dinner in the hotel restaurant, which he hoped would be included. Still, that sounded kind of lonely, and he actually hoped his number wasn't called.

"Here's the first winning number, Crawlers. Pay attention," Vic said. "Five nine two eight eight. That number again is five nine two eight eight. If that's your ticket number, come on up and claim your prize."

A woman squealed from the back of the crowd, and then made her way up to the stage as everyone clapped. Carter let out a relieved breath and looked at Ivy.

"Guess we're not lucky," Carter said.

"I don't know," Ivy replied. "Let's hear what the prize is."

The prize was a gift card to a local wine shop for a group wine tasting, and the winner's girlfriends all gave raucous cheers.

Ivy gave him a tight smile. "I'd say we're very lucky."

Carter laughed and watched as the woman shimmied her way through the crowd back to her friends, holding the gift card up high. It came as no surprise to him to see Lizzie trying to wedge herself into that group.

"Oh for God's sake," he said.

"You know her?" Ivy asked.

"I used to work with her. She's obnoxious."

"She's my best friend," Ivy said with a steady look.

Carter's face heated with his blush. "Oh, I..." He frowned and took a step closer. "Are you joking with me again?"

Ivy's expression didn't change as she said, "Yes. I'm joking with you."

"That's not very funny."

"Humor is very selective." She shifted her gaze to look over Carter's shoulder, and he turned, finding himself looking at the cartoon abs on Harry's T-shirt.

"Oh, pardon me," Harry said, and stepped around him, nodding to Ivy who stared at him.

"He was watching you," Ivy said, turning her attention back to Carter. "Standing behind you and looking at you."

Carter frowned and looked after Harry, noticing the man carried a drink in each hand. He figured one of the drinks would be for Lizzie, and hoped Harry would realize soon he should dial back Lizzie's intake of booze.

"Watching me in a creepy way?" Carter asked.

"I guess that would depend on what you think is creepy." She held up her empty glass. "I'm going to get another drink. Do you want something?"

"No, thanks though."

He watched Ivy move off through the crowd, her wings trailing over everyone she passed, and some of the feathers dipping into some drinks. Shifting his attention back toward Harry, Carter was surprised to see him hand one of his drinks to a handsome older man.

Apparently, someone appreciated Harry's hair, mustache, and casual attire. Good for him.

Another whine of feedback made the crowd flinch. Vic's voice rumbled over the sound system. "Sorry about the feedback, Crawlers. Too many fillings, I guess. I wanted to give you a heads up. In about ten minutes, we'll be getting on the shuttles and heading out to bar number two on our stop. Who knows what bar we're taking over next?"

"Intentions!" the majority of people shouted, and Carter was relieved that no one followed that up with, *A fag bar!* He apparently needed to give people more benefit of the doubt. Well, maybe he needed to do that for the Cupid Crawlers, as Vic called them, but probably not society as a whole.

Vic laughed at the response. "That's right! I'm glad to see you're still sober enough to know what the next bar is. Like I said, we have about ten minutes, so get in line now for the bathroom and slug down the last of whatever you're drinking. Come see me at the door for your shuttle assignment."

Many of the crowd headed for the bathrooms, but Carter decided he was pretty much done with That Corner Bar. There was no sign of Ivy or Harry, and thankfully Lizzie had dropped out of sight as well, so he approached Vic who stood near the exit. Vic smiled as Carter approached, his clipboard propped against his belly.

"Hello, Carter," Vic said. "How'd you enjoy the first stop on the Cupid Crawl?"

He gave a half shrug. "It was all right."

"Just all right, huh?" Vic pursed his lips. "Well, maybe the next bar will be more to your liking. I saw you talking to that girl Lizzie. You two seem pretty friendly."

"Not even a little bit," Carter said. "She's a nemesis from a previous job."

Vic laughed in surprise. "A nemesis?"

"Yep. She came up with a terrible nickname for me and everything."

"Is that so?"

"It is. Carter the Farter, isn't that mature?"

Vic tried to hide his grin, but failed spectacularly. "It is not mature. Not at all."

"Who calls people that?" Carter grumbled.

Vic's grin grew to a smirk. "No one in their right mind."

Carter narrowed his eyes. "You know what? Just tell me what shuttle to get on."

"You're on shuttle two," Vic said.

"Thank you." Carter moved toward the door.

"And the shuttle windows do open a bit, in case you need some fresh air during the drive," Vic said after him, and snorted a laugh that he tried to pull off as a cough.

"You're as bad as she is," Carter said.

He stepped outside and crossed his arms against the cold. Boarding his assigned shuttle, he gave the driver a quick nod in greeting. Carter took a window seat in the middle of the shuttle and unlocked his phone. He opened the Grindr app and started scrolling through the profiles listed nearby. A nice gathering of Grindr users were clustered inside That Corner Bar, and Carter looked through them.

Some definite possibilities had made themselves available. Carter tapped on those profiles that showed the user's face and read through the details provided. He sneered as he scrolled past his bathroom hook up, VersatileJoe75. More like Ifinishedb4U&leftUhangingJoe75.

People climbed on the shuttle, laughing and talking as they shrugged out of cupid wings in order to be able to sit. A young blond guy wearing a short sleeve polo shirt and nicely faded jeans pointed to the empty seat next to Carter.

"Anyone sitting here?" the guy asked.

"No, it's available," Carter said with a smile.

The guy sat and a gentle and pleasing scent wafted over Carter. It was as if he stood on a beach between the ocean and a shady wood.

"Aaron," the guy said, extending his hand.

Carter shook with him. "Carter." He nodded down to their clasped hands. "Not many people shake hands anymore."

"I guess my parents raised me right," Aaron said.

"Seems that way," Carter said. "But you did sit next to and start talking with a stranger."

"I may not have listened to everything my parents told me." Aaron's grin was sly and adorable.

"Well thank God for independent thinking." Carter returned Aaron's grin. "What brings you to the Cupid Crawl?"

"I came with a group of friends," Aaron said. "They're sitting in the back of the bus."

The doors closed and the shuttle pulled away from the curb. Carter craned his neck to look over his seat at the joking and laughing group in the back rows.

"Why aren't you sitting back there with them?" Carter asked.

"I'm odd man out," Aaron said with a shrug. "There are seven of us, so I decided to sit next to the guy who caught my eye in the bar earlier."

"Oh?" Carter smiled and made a show of sliding his phone into his pants pocket. "Guess I should put my Grindr scroll on hold for a bit."

Aaron's expression tightened, and he looked away. "Grindr, huh? I met my last boyfriend on that app." He flashed a quick, sad smile. "I lost him through it six months later."

"Ouch," Carter said. "Sorry about that."

"Are you profile CummingOutofTheBlue?"

Carter shook his head. "Nope. I'm CWSouthBoston955."

"That's good," Aaron said. "CummingOutofTheBlue was the profile responsible for ending my relationship."

Since they'd just introduced themselves, Carter decided not to point out that Aaron's boyfriend had actually been the one to end their relationship, and not the other Grindr profile. That kind of conversation was best had, oh, probably never.

"Anyway, it's nice to meet you, again. And that's why I'm not on Grindr. It's fine for some people, but I really like to talk to someone and get to know them before I have sex."

"I've found a few dates through the app," Carter said. "We went out before we had sex."

"So you didn't have sex on the first date?"

"Well, no, not really," Carter said as his cheeks heated. "We had sex on the first meetup, but we met someplace else first. So, technically, it was a date."

"Nice technicality."

"Did it convince you?"

"Of what? Your purity?"

Carter laughed, and Aaron chuckled as well.

"I'm glad you took that as a joke," Aaron said.

"I'm glad it was meant as a joke," Carter said. "Because, I really am quite pure."

"Uh-huh."

"I am. Ask anyone."

One of the other shuttles pulled up alongside the one they rode in. Aaron frowned as he looked past Carter.

"Is that someone you know?" Aaron asked.

Carter turned and found Lizzie laughing and pointing and waving at him. There was no sign of Harry, but whatever Lizzie was saying had gotten the rest of the shuttle riders laughing with her. Carter had a feeling he knew what she was saying, but he turned away from the window and smiled at Aaron.

"I barely know her," Carter said. "Pay her no mind."

"That whole shuttle seems to think she's pretty funny."

"She's drunk. They're all drunk. Drunk and ridiculous. That's the drunk as skunks shuttle. So, tell me about yourself. What do you do?"

For the rest of the ride they traded personal information. Aaron was a software engineer for a start-up company Carter had never heard of. When Carter told him he was a project manager, Aaron hissed and used his fingers to make a sign of the cross.

"Project Managers are the bane of my existence," Aaron said.

"Because you have a PM at work that keeps asking you when you think you'll be done with the thing you're working on?" Carter surmised.

"Exactly," Aaron said with a mock surprised expression. "It's almost as if you may have done the same thing yourself."

"Once or twice," Carter said. "Usually to a software engineer known for delivering his code behind schedule."

Aaron made a face. "Ouch."

"That wasn't directed at you," Carter said with a little too much sweetness in his voice.

"You've got an edge," Aaron said with a smirk. "I kind of like that."

"Yeah?" Carter smirked back. "I'm pleased to have made it past the initial interview. What's the next step?"

"You get to meet my friends," Aaron said. "And we can buy each other drinks."

"I'm sure your friends will love me."

"I'm sure they will, too."

The shuttle slowed to a stop and the driver opened the door. Everyone filed off and into the entrance of Intentions. It was a gay dance bar, and a song with a heavy bass line thumped over the sound system. Lights flashed and spun above the large dance floor, and Carter was surprised to see at least two dozen men already inside the bar, a good number of them dancing. Valentine's Day on a Friday really got people going.

He lost track of Aaron in the crowd, so he made his way to the bar and lingered there, hoping to see him. As he stood there, another shuttle arrived and people filed inside and past him. He looked for Ivy, Harry, and even Lizzie, but didn't see them. A few minutes later, Aaron approached with a few guys trailing after him. One of the guys was none other than his Grindr hook up in the bathroom of the last bar, VersatileJoe75.

Oh shit.

"Here you are," Aaron said with a smile.

Carter hoped his own smile looked more genuine than it felt. "Here I am."

"So these are my friends," Aaron said. "That's Joe—" He pointed to VersatileJoe75, and Carter exchanged a nod with the man. "This is Bill, and that's Yondu, and Satish, and Gerard, and David."

"Hello all." Carter gave a small wave, then looked at Aaron, took a breath, and said, "Actually, Joe and I have met."

"You don't have to..." Joe started.

"Oh?" Aaron looked between them, then his eyes widened and he turned to Joe as he pointed at Carter. "Is this the guy you hooked up with in the bathroom? The Hoover?"

Carter frowned. Had Joe used the term Hoover in a good sense, or a bad sense? And dear God, could this bar crawl get any more bizarre?

Joe's cheeks were so red they practically glowed as he gave Aaron one of the best death-ray glares Carter had seen in a while.

"Yes, this is the guy I met up with in the bathroom," Joe said.

"I believe all the kids are calling it 'hooking up'," Carter said. He gave a tight smile to the rest of the group before meeting Aaron's gaze. "I'll give you guys a chance to talk on your own. It was nice chatting with you on the shuttle, Aaron."

He turned and ran into someone standing directly behind him. A big and solid someone who lifted his hands to avoid spilling the two drinks he carried.

It was, of course, Harry.

"Sorry, Carter," Harry said. "I thought you were going to zig when you actually zagged."

"My fault, Harry," Carter said, managing to keep his irritation

THE CUPID CRAWL

at Joe and Aaron and the entire Stupid Crawl at a low boil. "I need to watch where I'm going."

"Let's share the blame on this one, how's that?" Harry suggested with a smile.

Carter nodded. "Sounds good."

Harry studied him a moment, then said, "Everything okay? You seem a little on edge. Well, a little more on edge than usual."

Than usual. As if Harry knew him well enough by now to know what his "usual" edginess was like.

A deep ache started low in his belly, and he realized it was from missing someone who truly knew him that well. Someone like Will.

"I'm fine," Carter said. "Just one thing after another it seems."

"You know today is supposed to be a fun way to meet new people, right?"

Carter crossed his arms and glared. "Oh? I hadn't realized that. Thanks for the overview."

Harry laughed and leaned down to say in a low, gruff voice, "I like your sharp edges, Carter. I think the right man could smooth those out, and you'd have a lot of fun in the process."

"Many men have tried and failed," Carter said, then made a face. "That makes me sound like a real slut."

"Well, I did interrupt your hook up in the men's room at the very first bar on the crawl."

"Ugh. Fine! I'm a slut, okay?"

The words came out a lot louder than what he'd imagined inside his head, and people five deep in the crowd turned to look. And standing just a few feet away was Ivy, black feathered wings trembling as she laughed. Carter stared at the floor and let out a long, slow breath as Harry laughed.

"Here," Harry finally said, gently bumping his hand against Carter's chest. "I think you need this more than I do."

Carter accepted the drink and sniffed it. "Whisky?"

"Crown Royal and 7 Up," Harry said.

Carter took a long drink and nodded as the whisky warmed his belly. "Thanks."

Harry took a step back, and looked at him with one eye closed before handing over the second drink, also a Crown and Seven from what Carter could tell.

"I can't take both your drinks," Carter said even as he accepted the second glass.

"You definitely need them more than we do."

"Lizzie's drinking Crown and Seven?" Carter frowned. "I thought she was more of a fruity drink connoisseur."

"Hell, I lost track of Lizzie on the shuttle," Harry said with a shrug. "I bought those for me and Brian."

"Is he that guy you were talking with at the last bar?" Carter asked.

"Yeah. He's pretty interesting." Harry looked at Carter a moment. "You want to come talk with us?"

"I wouldn't want to intrude," Carter said, taking a long swallow of the first drink Harry had given him and surprised to discover he had finished it.

"You wouldn't be intruding," Harry said. "Just don't make a play for Brian, and we'll be okay."

"Well, you know, no guarantees about that," Carter said with a chuckle that sounded more like a loud laugh once he got going. How strong was that drink? "I am a slut after all."

Harry smiled and reached out to take the untouched second drink from Carter's hand. "On second thought, I'm going to keep this for myself. How about you wait here and I'll bring you back a tall glass of water?"

"Yeah, probably a good idea."

Carter watched Harry merge into the crowd. He chewed on an ice cube from his glass, and danced in place as he people-watched the crowd.

"You seem happier."

Carter looked around to find Ivy standing behind him, smirking as she held a silver flask close to her body.

"I just had a drink," Carter said.

"I saw," Ivy said. "A drink that tall guy with the twisted-ended mustache and big hands gave you. The one who was looking you over at the first bar."

"Are you trying to get inside my head and freak me out?" Carter asked.

"No." She leaned in closer and lowered her voice. "But is it working?"

"You're an interesting Angel of Death."

"Thanks." Ivy sipped from her flask, then held it toward him. "Want some?"

Carter eyed the flask suspiciously. "What is it?"

"Something I smuggled in from home."

"Well, duh. But what is it?"

She pulled the flask back, sipped again, capped it, and then slipped it out of sight into an inside pocket of her velvet jacket. "It's my own home brew."

"Uh huh."

Carter's phone buzzed in his pocket, and he pulled it free to find a text from Will waiting for him.

You able to talk?

"Is that your boyfriend?" Ivy asked.

"No," Carter said, looking around for a place to talk to Will. "Well, he was for a hot minute, but we decided we were better friends than lovers."

Ivy made a face. "Lovers? Does anyone say lover anymore?"

Carter gave her a gentle glare. "I must be behind the times."

She shrugged one shoulder, the wing behind it shifting in time. "At least you're dressed fancy."

"I'm going to find a place to talk on the phone."

"Okay. See you around."

Carter made his way through the crowd, looking this way and that. He spotted a set of French doors that opened onto a walled-in garden patio and headed that direction. Since it was so cold, only a small group of smokers were outside, shoulders hunched and huddled together for warmth as they puffed cigarettes. Carter stepped through one of the doors, gasping at the bite of the frigid air. The smokers regarded him with something like suspicion as he moved to a corner of the garden away from them. He ignored them and placed a FaceTime video call to Will. The brick walls of the patio blocked the full force of the wind, but he still shivered in the cold air as he waited for Will to answer.

"Hey there," Will said, sweat standing out on his face, and his smile bright inside his dark blond beard. He frowned as he looked at Carter's surroundings. "Are you outside again?"

"Yeah, on the patio at Intentions."

"Isn't it cold?"

"For you, I will brave the Arctic breath of winter."

Will's frown deepened. "How drunk are you?"

"Sober enough to know better than to tell you what I've had to drink," Carter said, then tried to follow his own logic and ended up making a face that matched Will's confused expression. "Anyway, enough about me and our Boston winter. How are things down there? Why are you sweaty?"

"Because it's hot and crowded in this room backstage," Will said. "Though they do have a nice spread of food and drinks."

"Oh, show me!"

Will turned the phone to show off long tables populated by bowls and platters of food, and a wide variety of beverages. A number of people milled around the tables, all of them dressed nicely and talking and laughing.

"Holy shit, it's like you're at the Grammy's!" Carter said.

Will turned the phone around again to be able to see Carter. "I know!"

"Has Rex's award category been announced yet?"

"No, that's later," Will said. "The performers are doing sound checks, and stuff like that. He's onstage doing a sound check for his song, so I decided to check in with you. How's the Cupid Crawl?"

"Oh, you know how these things are," Carter said.

"No, I don't. Why don't you tell me?"

"Ugh. Fine. I've met some... interesting people."

"Other than Dizzy Frizzy Lizzie?" Will asked.

"Yes, other than her. There's this kind of odd girl named Ivy who's dressed all in black and wearing wings made out of black feathers."

"Does she know it's not Halloween?"

"Yeah, she knows. She's kind of like a Goth Cupid."

"Is she nice?"

Carter shook his head. "Not at all. She's sarcastic and has a sense of humor as dry as the Sahara."

"You must be in Heaven," Will said with a smirk.

"You know it." Carter glanced toward the smokers. A couple of the guys were watching him, so he smiled but turned away and lowered his voice. "There are quite a few guys on Grindr here. I connected with one of them, and we, um, introduced ourselves in a stall in the bathroom."

Will's eyes widened. "You did it in a bathroom stall?"

"Who did?"

The question came from someone on Will's end who stood offscreen. Rex moved into view behind Will and peered over his shoulder at the phone.

"Carter, my man," Rex said with a smirk. "Gettin' yourself some Valentine's Day jostle and tussle? Nice."

"Jostle and tussle?" Carter said.

Will gave Rex a quick kiss then moved out of the room to somewhere apparently less crowded.

"Sorry about that," Will said. "I didn't know Rex had come up beside me."

"Oh, that's fine." Carter shrugged, and it turned into a shiver. "I've already announced I'm a slut to a quarter of the people here."

"Way to sell yourself."

"I know, right? So what's jostle and tussle?"

Will smirked. "It's Rex's phrase for sex."

"Sounds more like a wrestling match," Carter said.

"Believe me, it can be like that sometimes." Will's smirk turned into a full-blown smile, and a blush blossomed in his cheeks.

"Well, well, well, look at you, all sexed up by your hot husband."

"Yeah, look at me, all sweaty and anxious in the middle of a bunch of in shape and talented music industry types."

"Hey, stop that right now," Carter snapped, and was glad to see Will jump a bit. "You are a smart, caring, handsome man, and you deserve whatever makes you happy."

"Aw, thank—"

"And if you get off by wriggling into a wrestling singlet, and squaring off against your husband until you're both sweaty and hard as rocks, after which you strip each other down and flip-flop fuck yourselves senseless, well? More power to you, my friend. You grab yourself a handful of happy, no matter how hard or soft it is, and you work it until it spews joy juice all over you."

Will stared at his phone with wide eyes.

"That was a very, um, detailed affirmation," Will said. "Thank you?"

"You're welcome." Carter brushed some hair off his forehead, and watched as the smokers filed back into the bar, leaving him on his own.

"So, just curious here, but when you mentioned hooking up with someone in a bathroom stall, did you both, you know, um, to borrow your phrase, spew your joy juice?"

Carter clenched his jaw a moment before responding. "I'm not sure why you're asking me such a personal question."

"It just seems like you got a little, shall I say, worked up, with that affirmation."

Carter huffed and his breath clouded around the phone. "Well, if you must know, I performed such a memorable blowjob, the guy gave me the nickname Hoover to his buddies. And, no, I did not get a chance to complete my end of the transaction."

"I see... Hoover." Will grinned. "I think you need to get yourself some jostle and tussle before too long."

"Ha ha," Carter said with a sneer that turned into a genuine smile. "Seriously, though, I'm glad you're having fun."

"Yeah, it's not as bad as I'd feared," Will said with a half shrug. "But I do wish I was able to be there to keep you company and, apparently, stand guard outside bathroom stalls to make sure you get a chance to, how did you put it?"

"Complete my end of the transaction," Carter said with a sigh.

"Right. That." Will moved the phone close enough for his face to fill the screen, and he lowered his voice. "You okay, Cartier?"

"I'm okay, Big Willie." Despite the cold, a warm feeling flared into life low in the center of his chest. "You just take care of yourself and your handsome singer husband, and when you get home Sunday, I will regale you with tales of my jostling and tussling."

"I look forward to the regaling."

They shared a smile, then Carter shivered again. "I should get back inside before I end up like Jack Nicholson at the end of *The Shining*."

"I hope the day gets better," Will said.

A light tap on the glass of the patio door pulled Carter's attention, and he saw Harry peering out at him and holding up a large glass of ice water. Carter laughed and nodded.

"What's so funny?" Will asked.

"Oh, just someone checking in on me," Carter said, looking back at his phone. "You take care, Big Willie."

"You first, Cartier."

"Love you, my friend."

"Love you back. Talk to you soon."

Carter ended the video call and hurried toward the doors. Harry saw him coming and pushed down on the handle on his side, but the door didn't budge. Harry stared wide-eyed at Carter through the glass and jiggled the door handle several times.

"Oh my God, are you fucking kidding me?" Carter said, arms crossed tight across his chest. "I'm freezing!"

Harry grinned and, with a final, slow push of the handle, popped the patio door open. A rush of warm air enveloped Carter, as well as the sound of the crowd and thump of music. Carter stepped inside and gave Harry a narrow-eyed look.

"That wasn't funny," Carter said.

Harry smiled and handed him the ice water. "I beg to differ. And this should cool you down."

"I'm cool enough, thanks," Carter said.

He sipped his water and glared at Harry's back as the big man ambled off through the crowd. Some people thought they were so hilarious.

But even as he glared at Harry, Carter caught himself checking out the round, firm swell of Harry's ass inside his stonewashed jeans. Not that he was at all interested in the man, but, damn, Harry must be a master at squats.

CHAPTER SEVEN

Carter lingered near the patio doors because a vent above him was pushing out warm air. He lost sight of Harry in the crowd, so he stood under the gentle flow of heat and sipped his water. Harry had invited Carter to join him and Brian for conversation, but Carter didn't want to be a third wheel. His talk with Will had helped, and he felt better about being on his own.

Still, Harry's ass had looked good as he'd walked away.

He finished the water and threaded his way through the crowd, dodging wings and more than a few stumbling cupids. Apparently, the majority of Crawlers needed to be drinking more water. They were only at the second bar; didn't these people understand how to pace themselves?

He set his empty glass on the end of the bar, and had started for the bathroom when the music volume dropped and Vic's voice boomed over a microphone.

"Who wants pizza?"

Raucous cheers went up, and Vic laughed.

"I've heard from the pizza place, and they're finishing up our order and will have the pizzas here within thirty minutes. There's meat lovers—"

Another round of cheers.

"—vegetarian—"

A quiet round of cheers, mostly drowned out by booing from what Carter assumed was the meat lovers in the crowd.

"—and gluten and dairy free options."

"Why fucking bother?" a man shouted, and everybody laughed.

"Diversity is the spice of life," Vic said. "To repeat, pizzas will be here in thirty minutes and set up over by the patio doors. We're here at Intentions until 1:30, and then we'll board the shuttles for the next bar. Who knows the name of that one?"

Carter had no memory of the name of the next bar, but several people shouted it out.

"Hip Check!"

Carter remembered it now: a sports bar. He made a face as he continued to the restroom. There was a line just inside the door, so he distracted himself by looking through Grindr. Several profiles were active within the bar, and a couple showed as being just a few feet away. He covertly checked out the guys around him, and tried to match the men he saw up with a profile. That was the trouble with Grindr: some guys didn't provide a picture of their face. Any number of shots of their dick, but nothing of their face. Carter understood the privacy concern, but he had a couple of pictures showing his face on his own profile, and he tried to limit his connections to other guys on the app who did the same.

"You CWSouthBoston955?"

Carter turned to find a familiar man standing in line behind him. This was the man he'd talked to at That Corner Bar who'd stuck a suction-cup-tipped arrow to Carter's forehead. Frank, that was his name.

"That's me," Carter said. "And you're Frank, right?"

"Right," Frank said with a smile, then held up his phone. "And also 617SoxFan4Ever."

"Sox fan forever, huh? White Sox?" Carter asked, knowing full well Frank's Grindr name referred to the Boston Red Sox, especially since he'd included the original Boston area code at the beginning.

Frank leveled a cool look at him. "Red Sox."

Carter grinned. "I knew that."

From the look he received, it didn't appear that Frank believed him.

"You must be looking forward to the next bar," Carter said.

Frank shrugged. "It's more of a hockey bar than baseball."

"Sports bars are that specific now?"

"It's not like they only show hockey on the televisions," Frank said. "But it depends on the season. Since it's February, there's no baseball going on. But the bulk of the memorabilia on display is hockey related."

Carter decided he'd had enough of sports related conversation, so opted for a different track, and gestured to the red fanny pack Frank wore.

"Have you emptied your quiver?"

"That's a very personal question," Frank said with a grin, then nodded past Carter. "You're up."

Carter stepped up to an open urinal and sighed with relief. When he'd finished, he washed his hands and left the restroom. It had been nice talking with Frank, but Carter didn't want to seem too clingy, so he merged back into the crowd. There were four more bars to go; he'd get another chance to talk with Frank before the end of the day.

After checking his Grindr app a few times, Carter decided to try the old fashioned routine of simply talking with people. First, though, he needed a drink. The Crown and Seven Harry had bought him had been good, very good. But he didn't want to get too drunk too fast, especially with Lizzie lurking in the crowd, just waiting to pop up behind him like something out of a horror movie and shout, "Farter!"

He ordered a bottled beer and as he turned away from the bar, stopped when he caught sight of Harry. The man was talking and laughing with a pretty woman, and as Carter watched, she put a hand on Harry's forearm and leaned in close to say something. Harry's laugh boomed through the bar, even managing to be heard over the heavy bass of the music.

Well, Harry was really making the rounds. Which is exactly what Carter should be doing. And he didn't want to give much thought to the feeling in his chest, like the tiniest little twist of... what? Not jealousy, not for Harry after having only talked with him a few times. Something a bit different from that.

He pulled his gaze away from Harry—avoiding checking out the man's ass this time—and looked at his phone. There were some promising profiles on Grindr, and he sent a message to one of them: *Hey fellow Crawler.*

A moment later, the guy wrote back: *Hey. Want to meet up?*

Carter smiled to himself and responded: *Fuck yeah. Last stall in the bathroom?*

Ten minutes, came the reply.

Carter finished his beer and made his way to the bathroom. The end stall was empty and he stepped in. Leaving the door open, he turned his back and pretended to be peeing.

"You order a meet up?"

Carter turned and smiled. The guy was cute, with blond hair, a scruff of golden beard, and the body of an underwear model. Hot damn, jackpot! Here was his chance to get some jostle and tussle of his own.

Well, seeing as how they were meeting up in a public area with limited space, it might only be a bit of jostle.

His hook up stepped into the stall and locked the door behind him. They kissed, and Carter reached down to squeeze the steadily hardening length in his jeans.

"Enjoying the crawl?" Carter asked.

"Less talk," the guy said, and unzipped his jeans. "More action."

"Okay then."

Determined not to get left in the lurch once again, Carter unzipped his own pants. He and the hot guy pulled their dicks out at the same time, and Carter took both in one hand and slowly stroked. Pre-cum slicked their hot shafts, and Hot Guy surprised Carter by leaning in for a kiss. He'd seemed more of the let's-get-off-and-move-along type, and not someone into the more passionate side of sex like kissing.

But, damn, Hot Guy was a good kisser.

Carter released his own cock and took hold of Hot Guy's dick. More kissing, and Hot Guy returned the favor, stroking Carter. He knew what he was doing, adding a quick twist of his hand around the head of Carter's prick. Carter mimicked the move, figuring it was how Hot Guy jerked himself off. He was rewarded with a deep moan, and then Hot Guy paused in the middle of a kiss, mouth open and eyes closed as Carter moved his hand faster, still twisting at the top.

"Yeah, I'm there," Hot Guy gasped. He stopped stroking and gripped Carter tight. "I'm close. I'm really close. I'm right... there."

Hot Guy turned his hips toward the toilet and seconds later the cock bucked against Carter's palm. Cum splashed into the water and around the porcelain rim. Carter squeezed the last drops out and shook them off the tip. Hot Guy leaned in for a quick kiss, then smiled as he resumed his strokes.

Carter closed his eyes and braced himself against the walls of the stall. Finally, he was going to come.

Someone rushed into the bathroom. The new arrival smacked a hand on the door of the stall where Hot Guy was working Carter's dick. Hot Guy jumped and lost his grip on Carter.

"Occupied!" Carter snapped.

"Sorry... oh!" The guy banged into the neighboring stall and slammed the door. In seconds, his pants had dropped around his ankles and he produced sounds that Carter was certain no other human being had ever managed.

"Oh my God," Hot Guy said, and snorted a laugh. "I'm sorry, I can't... I gotta leave."

"What? Wait!"

But it was too late, Hot Guy had already opened the door and fled.

The guy in the next stall moaned and made more horrible noises. It sounded as if some kind of monstrosity from another dimension was crawling out of guy's ass. Carter glared at the metal wall separating them and flipped the guy off with both hands, despite his intestinal distress.

Carter put himself back together, straightened his shoulders, and stepped out of the stall. He really shouldn't have been surprised to find Harry standing at the sink, washing his hands. Was Harry following him around and listening in on his hook ups?

"Hello," Carter said, approaching a sink and washing his hands. "Imagine finding you in the men's room."

"Round two?" Harry asked with a knowing smile.

The guy in the stall groaned, and Carter decided he'd had enough.

"I gotta get out of here," he said and strode past Harry to the door.

After stepping out of the men's room, a traffic jam of bodies—most wearing some kind of angel wings—stopped Carter in his tracks. The hallway was narrow, and Carter had become trapped by the line for the women's room and the line at the bar. A man behind him cleared his throat, and Carter was surprised to find Harry standing just over his shoulder. Fighting back an eye roll, Carter managed a tight smile.

"I see you haven't earned any wings yet," Carter said.

Harry's eyebrows went up. "Are they giving away wings?"

"No, I was just making a comment... Never mind."

They were silent a moment, then Harry leaned down and whispered in Carter's ear, "How was it this time?"

Carter pursed his lips and crossed his arms. "How's that woman you were talking with?"

"Nice deflection," Harry said. "And she's very nice. Her name is Charlotte."

"Like the spider?"

"Manners, Carter."

Harry's voice held a note of amusement, and all Carter wanted at that moment was to be as far away from the man as possible. A gap opened in the crowd and he darted forward, hoping he'd managed to leave Harry behind.

Alas, the man was quick as well as annoying, because he was hot on Carter's heels. Try as he might to forge a path away from Harry, Carter ended up stranded by the crowd once again, this time standing beside Harry as he reconnected with Charlotte. To Carter's surprise, the handsome older man from the first bar, whose name was Brian if Carter remembered correctly, stood at Harry's side opposite Charlotte.

Harry was apparently working both sides of the gender aisle today. Carter had to admit he was impressed. If he wasn't feeling a bit off his game, he'd probably be talking with more people himself. Or at least he should be.

"And here he is, as if I summoned him," Harry said. "Everyone, this is Carter, who I was telling you about before excusing myself."

Carter turned and found a group of people smiling at him, a

mix of men and women. Damn, Harry was really playing the room! Along with Brian and Charlotte, there were four more people, two women and two men, all of them, like Charlotte, wearing harnesses with red feathered wings on their backs.

"Hello," Carter said, and gave a small wave. "Don't mind me. Just trying to wedge myself through the crowd. Please, go on with your discussion."

Harry laughed. "Join us, Carter. You might enjoy it."

"Well..." Carter looked around but saw no sign of Lizzie. He supposed he could do worse than being chatted up by a group of smiling people. "Okay, sure."

Harry introduced Carter to everyone, the names quickly leaving Carter's mind even though he attempted to retain them. Charlotte started talking about a couple of movies she'd seen recently, neither of which Carter was familiar with, so he stood and listened, trying to decipher whether the group was made up of friends who were all single, or if one or more of them were in a relationship.

"Figure it out yet?" Harry had leaned down and lowered his voice so that only Carter could hear him.

"Figure what out yet?" Carter asked.

"Who in their group is with who?"

"Oh, I didn't really try to..."

Harry raised his eyebrows and grinned. "Really? You weren't standing there trying to pair them up?"

"Did you do that?"

"Of course I did," Harry said with a laugh.

"What are you two talking about?" one of the women asked, and Carter thought her name was Melinda.

"Nothing..." Carter started to say.

"Which of you is sleeping with the other," Harry said and smiled big enough to lift the tips of his mustache.

Melinda and the rest of the group laughed, then she pointed

to one of the guys who had brown curly hair and a three-day scruff of beard. "Ron and I have an open relationship." She put an arm around Charlotte who stood next to her. "And Charlotte here likes to fill our openings."

"Scott and I are married," the third woman in the group said, waving toward a red headed man with thinning hair and glasses. "But we've dabbled with having a third now and then."

Brian, the older man Harry had been talking with previously, smirked and looked at Harry. "Ah, to be young again."

"I don't know," Harry said with a shrug. "I learned a lot of shit in my youth. Kind of nice to be done with that crap and know what I really want."

"And what is it you really want?" Brian asked.

"Someone to laugh with," Harry said, then turned to Carter. "How about you, Carter? What are you looking for?"

"From what I've heard, it's someone to hook up with," Melinda said and arched an eyebrow at Carter. "Or am I wrong?"

Carter fought back a wave of defensiveness and smiled. "Must be a slow news day if people are talking about my sex life."

"Earlier you did practically shout that you were acting slutty," Harry said with a shrug.

"True." Carter nodded and looked at Melinda. "I like to have fun, sure. But I'm also looking to find someone special. I think that's what most people want, isn't it? Open relationships are fine if both parties are on the same page. No matter how many people are in a relationship, two or three or more, it's nice if there's a connection there. Something deeper. Hooking up is fun, and I'm on Grindr a lot, I admit it, but that doesn't mean I want to do it for the rest of my life."

"You're looking for a husband?" asked the ginger with thinning hair.

Carter shrugged. "I'm looking for someone I like to spend

more than an afternoon with, someone to last beyond the jostle and tussle."

Harry laughed. "Jostle and tussle? Is that your phrase for sex?"

"I heard it from a friend recently," Carter said. "It seemed to fit. Anyway, I do hook up with guys from Grindr, and if one of them turns into something permanent, that would be great." He nodded, then gestured toward the bar. "I think I'm going to get myself a drink, and hang out by the tables so I can get a piece of pizza while it's hot."

He shot Harry a quick smile before turning away and approaching the bar. As he waited in line, Carter checked out Grindr, but after a short time, returned his phone to his pocket. Melinda's statement had irked him, he had to admit. It lodged in his craw like a large, bitter pill he'd failed to swallow. He wasn't ashamed of his sexuality or libido, but he didn't want people spreading rumors about him. Especially if they had never even met him before.

Though if he'd really done the deed—and twice today at that—could he call it a rumor?

"Penny for your thoughts."

Carter jumped. Harry stood behind him, smiling, the lights hanging over the bar reflecting in the lenses of his glasses.

"Not thinking much of anything," Carter said.

"Somehow I doubt that. You seem to be a pretty thoughtful person."

"Well, everyone's entitled to an opinion," Carter said, and flinched when he heard the defensive tone in his voice. "Sorry. I didn't mean to snap at you."

Harry shrugged. "It's okay. I know you're not mad at me. I mean, I'm a fucking bundle of joy to be around, so there's no way you could be mad at me."

Carter snorted a laugh. "You should get business cards printed up."

"I like that idea. Think I may steal it, if that's okay with you."

"It's all yours," Carter said.

"That'll make it official." Harry nodded toward the bar. "You're up."

"Oh, thanks." Carter approached the bar and asked for a bottled beer, then looked over his shoulder at Harry. "What do you want, FBJ?" He turned back to the bartender. "That's short for fucking bundle of joy."

The bartender smiled and gave Harry a quick once over. "I can see it."

Harry laughed. "Crown and Seven, please."

Carter paid, handed Harry his drink, and they stepped off to the side. The first sip of beer was much less sweet than the Crown and Seven, and Carter made a face that raised Harry's eyebrows.

"That bad?" Harry asked, then lifted his glass. "You should have stuck with the Crown and Seven."

"As good as those are, I'd be a super sloppy drunk before we got to the next bar."

Lizzie staggered up and fell against Harry. Her hair was a frizzy mess that she continually blew away from her face.

"Speaking of which..." Carter said.

"Hi boys!" Lizzie practically shouted at them. "Didja get any pizza?"

"It's not here yet," Harry said. "But when it does arrive, you should definitely have at least two pieces."

Lizzie blew a raspberry that reeked of booze, and waved Harry's suggestion away. The wave morphed into frantic swiping at the hair covering half her face until she managed to tuck it behind her ears. Her eyes were glassy and face slack as she pushed off of Harry and swayed on her feet. When she had steadied herself, she gave a nod.

"I'm going to go have a tinkle." She turned toward the

restrooms, then looked over her shoulder at Carter. "Smell you later!"

Her cackle could be heard above the thumping music as she swayed toward the bathroom.

"Such a delicate flower," Carter said.

"I had no idea what I was in for," Harry said with a shake of his head. "I didn't have any plans today, and decided it would be good to get out and meet some new people because I've been in a bit of a dating rut."

"Oh? I would have thought you'd have a wide open field," Carter said.

"Because I'm pan? While I see the logic in it, I still need to find someone I'm interested in getting to know better, no matter their gender or gender identity."

"Does that mean it's more complicated?" Carter held up a hand, palm out. "It's a serious question. I really want to know."

"In some ways it is," Harry replied. "Because there are a number of people who don't really understand what it means to be pan. Once we're through that part of the introductions, then I have to gauge whether I want to put in the work to know them any better."

"So it's like any other dating, only it involves some more initial setup? Are you saying you're like the IKEA version of sexual identity?"

Harry let out a booming laugh and put a hand on Carter's shoulder, giving him a gentle squeeze. "I've never heard it explained quite that way before, but I like it."

Ivy materialized out of the crowd, pale skin glowing beneath a recessed ceiling light.

"I'm sorry, the two of you are having entirely too much fun," Ivy said in a deadpan tone.

"Apologies, Angel of Death," Carter said, then gestured between Harry and Ivy. "Harry, this is Ivy. Ivy, this is Harry."

"You are the most somber Cupid I've seen today," Harry said. "Well done."

"Finally, someone who appreciates my vision," Ivy said.

Harry sipped his drink and returned his attention to Carter. "So what's your back story?"

"Oh yes," Ivy said, and fixed Carter with an intense stare. "Tell us your back story."

"My back story?"

"Yeah," Harry said. "What kind of relationships have you had?"

"What?"

"Have you had any lovers?" Ivy said, slowly enunciating each word. She looked at Harry and shook her head. "This young generation never listens."

Thoughts of Phillip barged into Carter's mind. The laughing and touching and snuggling and sex had all coalesced into what seemed like a single day, even though it had been six months. To Carter, his time with Phillip was similar to how a piece of coal became a diamond. The first six months had compressed into a single shiny and precious memory, as if all the good times had happened on one day. The last three months they'd been together, when Phillip had become more distant and started spending less time with Carter, seemed to make up the bulk of their time together. Phillip had blamed his distance and late hours on a busy time at work, but Carter had discovered the anonymous hook ups, and the money missing from his bank account. He'd been all set to break up in person, but Phillip had beat him to the punch and done it over text. When Carter had demanded his money back, Phillip had ghosted him.

It hadn't been much money overall, maybe five hundred dollars, but Carter had trusted Phillip, and that had been what hurt the most.

"Sorry, did I get too personal?" Harry asked.

Carter blinked and found Harry standing before him, an expression of concern wrinkling his forehead. Ivy stood beside Harry, looking concerned as well.

"You got too personal," Ivy said, and nudged Harry. "You're moving too fast, sasquatch. Ease up."

"No no," Carter said. "It's fine. Really. I just got caught up thinking about someone. Sorry, I mean something."

Harry and Ivy exchanged looks as the music volume lowered. Before Carter could say anything to try and salvage the situation, Vic's voice crackled over the PA system. "Pizza's ready! Eat up, Crawlers!"

The crowd surged toward the tables where the pizza boxes waited, Ivy vanishing into the horde as well. Carter took a long drink from his beer and leaned in toward Harry. "I'm going to wash my hands before I eat."

"I didn't mean to upset you," Harry said.

"You didn't. Really. I'll catch up with you in a little while."

Carter lifted his bottle in a farewell salute and turned toward the bathrooms. The powerful reaction to his memories of Phillip surprised him. All of that had happened over a year ago, and he'd thought he was over it. Apparently, some words were keys to opening up that Phillip door. Words like 'relationship' or 'love' or 'lover' or other such nonsense. And it should have come as no surprise that someone had asked him for the history of his love life during a bar crawl on Valentine's Day. Duh.

The bathroom was blissfully empty and Carter peed, washed his hands, and then gulped down what remained of his beer. He rinsed out the bottle at the sink and filled it with cold tap water. It was a trick he used to do long ago when he'd been broke and going to the bars. He'd buy himself one beer and keep filling the bottle with tap water throughout the night. It kept him sober, and helped him avoid spending too much money on beer. Another bonus, if he set the bottle down to go dance, the bus boys wouldn't take it if it felt full. And, with four more bars to go on the Cupid Crawl, he was going to need to pace himself.

He caught his own gaze in his reflection and stared. The possibility of escaping back to his apartment hung in the back of his mind. It wasn't too late to summon a Lyft to return home and see if he could line up some Grindr guys. Maybe one or two of his favorites were still available.

But, really, he could meet up with some Grindr guys right there on the crawl. Talk with them, get to know them a bit before running off to a bathroom stall together.

You might as well be dating them, a voice whispered in the back of his mind, but he ignored it.

The next bar would be the deciding factor. If he managed to have a halfway decent time at a sports bar—heavily decorated in hockey memorabilia, according to Frank—then Carter would stick it out for the remainder of the crawl.

CHAPTER EIGHT

Carter looked around the interior of Hip Check and nodded to himself. Frank had been right: the memorabilia on display leaned overwhelmingly in favor of hockey. He made his way to the bar and ordered a bottled beer. His old trick had worked well at Intentions, so he decided to continue with it.

All around him, Cupid Crawlers were steadily becoming more and more intoxicated. Carter was glad Vic had provided pizza at the last bar to help soak up some of the booze, but he realized he would need to choose his seat on the next shuttle ride more carefully to avoid any potential puke splatter.

He had dodged Harry and his new group of friends as well as Ivy the last hour at Intentions. Instead, after scarfing down a couple pieces of mediocre pizza off in a corner, he'd found a spot on the dance floor and relived the days of his past when he'd been hitting the bars more regularly. Back in college, he'd gone to the bars a lot more often, and often ended up going out on the dance floor alone for his favorite songs.

It had felt good to just let go and move to an upbeat song once again. He couldn't remember the last time he'd danced, even in his own apartment. That was something he needed to do more often. Sometimes the simplest things could make the biggest impact on his mood.

"I thought you might have taken off."

It was Frank, still looking hot in his tight red satin shorts, sparkly red fanny pack, and white wings strapped around his broad shoulders. Carter's gaze was drawn to the patch of fine blond hair between Frank's firm square pecs, and then to the tattoos around each shoulder before he met Frank's gaze.

"Take off and miss seeing the legendary Hip Check sports bar?" Carter looked around with exaggeratedly wide eyes. "Just look at all the hockey memorabilia in here."

Frank grinned and shook his head. "You're a bit of a smart ass, aren't you?"

"Says the man dressed as Cupid, and smacking suction-cup-tipped arrows onto people," Carter said.

"Just so you know, I've only given out three arrows today."

"So far," Carter said.

Frank nodded. "So far. But I would think that would get me some points."

"And now we're back to the sports theme of the bar."

"You're a real piece of work," Frank said.

"Thank you."

"That wasn't really a compliment."

Carter smiled. "I know."

"Do you know how to play pool?" Frank asked.

Carter shrugged. "I know how to play. Whether or not I'm good at it is a different story."

"Want to go check out the pool table in the back?"

"All right, yeah. Lead the way."

Carter followed Frank, staring at the shiny material of the shorts stretched tight over his ass. He really was a hot man, but Carter was having trouble getting a fix on whether or not Frank would be open to a quick hook up. With his thoughts meandering toward sex, and his gaze fixed on Frank's hot ass, he was caught off guard when the man stopped abruptly. Carter bumped into Frank, both of them stumbling forward a couple of steps.

"Sorry," Carter said, and moved to Frank's side. "Why'd you stop so... Oh."

Harry stood at the pool table, smiling at Carter and Frank as he chalked up a stick. Brian was racking the balls, the light over the table bringing out the silver threaded through his thick dark hair.

"You guys feeling lucky?" Harry asked.

"I was," Carter said.

"Up for a game of doubles?" Harry said, either not having heard Carter's comment or deciding to ignore it.

"I really don't think—" Carter started.

"Sure, we'll play you," Frank said over him.

Carter gave a heavy mental sigh. It must have showed in his expression because he caught Harry smirking at him.

"What?" Carter asked, not very surprised to hear the heightened level of irritation in his tone.

Harry's eyebrows went up and he pursed his lips. "So much aggression. It's almost like you're scared to play against me." Harry looked at Frank. "I get it now. He's scared I'll show him up in front of you, and ruin his chances with you."

Carter glared at Harry, but could see Frank grinning at him from the corner of his eye.

"Is that true?" Frank asked. "You afraid he's going to show you up?"

"Nope," Carter said, keeping his gaze fixed on Harry. "Not even a little bit. I'll just select my pool cue of destiny. Out of the way, castoff from *Land of the Giants*."

"Oh, damn, trash talk already?" Harry said with a hearty laugh. "And some really old school trash talk at that. What the hell streaming service are you watching, Carter, to toss out a TV show that old?"

"You're the one who obviously knows what I'm talking about," Carter shot back. "So if you want to talk about being old, well…"

Harry, Frank, and Brian all laughed. As Harry and Brian introduced themselves to Frank, Carter selected a stick from the wall rack. He chalked up the tip as Frank browsed through the remaining sticks.

"Don't let him get to you, guys," Brian said. "We barely crushed the previous teams we played."

Harry laughed, and when Carter finished chalking his stick, he blew across the tip and fixed Harry with a challenging look.

"Who breaks?" Carter asked.

Harry waved toward the table. "Since I invited you to play, I invite you to break."

Carter, in turn, waved Frank toward the table. "You're the only one of us wearing wings, so it's only fair that you break."

Frank set the cue ball and bent over. Carter smiled as the women and men standing behind Frank all cocked their heads and checked out his ass at the same time. Frank slowly slid the pool cue between his fingers as he took aim, and Carter thought he'd never seen anything quite as erotic in relation to pool. The loud impact of the cue ball against the racked balls snapped him out of his reverie, and he watched as a striped ball thunked into the side pocket. Frank gave him a wink as he moved around the table to line up his next shot.

Carter was impressed. Frank had nearly shattered the first ball in the group, and he'd already sunk one of their balls.

Harry moved up beside Carter and muttered, "He's pretty damn good. You might not even have to take a shot if he keeps it up."

"Wouldn't that be nice?" Carter said.

"Not a lover of pool?"

"It's fine," Carter said. "But not what I thought I'd be doing today."

"What, getting to know a few people during a bar crawl? Or were you looking forward to some no strings attached jostle and tussle, to use your term?"

Carter assessed Harry's smirk, then asked, "Are you trying to get my goat?"

"I think your goat is perfect just the way it is," Harry said. "I would never try to imprison your goat."

Frank missed his third shot and shrugged as he stepped back from the table. Harry leaned down to whisper to Carter, "And, for the record, the saying 'get my goat' is another example of you being an old man trapped in a young, hot body."

He stepped away to take his shot before Carter had a chance to reply. Frank stood beside him, but Carter ignored him as he watched Harry sink two solid balls before he missed.

"Your turn, old man," Harry said, bowing and waving toward the table.

Carter did a couple of quick squats then cracked his neck and knuckles. The routine got a smirk from Frank and Brian, and a full-fledged laugh out of Harry, which made him smile. He assessed the layout of the balls, decided on his shot, and leaned in over the table to take aim at a ball near the corner pocket.

Before taking the shot, however, he turned his head slightly and said to Harry standing behind him, "Stop staring at my ass, Harry."

"But it's so perky," Harry protested. "I can't look away."

Carter huffed a laugh before knocking the ball in. He tried for a second ball and missed. Moving back to allow Brian to take a shot, Carter ended up beside Frank who held out his fisted hand. Carter bumped it with his own as he watched Brian line up a shot. Raising his gaze, he caught Harry staring at him, but when their eyes met, Harry quickly looked away.

As the game went on, Carter ended up standing next to Harry more often than he did Frank. He and Harry exchanged gentle barbs and snarky remarks, usually so caught up in their own insults they had to be reminded to take their turns.

Harry and Brian won the game, and Carter and Frank were graceful losers. As they all put away the pool cues, Harry waved a waitress over and offered to buy everyone a round of drinks. Carter ordered a bottled beer while the other three opted for shots.

"We're only halfway through the crawl," Carter said as he shook his head.

"Don't judge us," Harry said, and crossed his arms as he stuck out his lower lip in a defiant pout.

"The maturity level on display is astounding," Carter said.

The waitress brought the drinks and Carter took a long pull from his beer as the other three threw back their shots. Harry collected the three shot glasses and turned away to set them on the tray of a passing waitress. When he turned back, he directed a big smile at Carter.

"Darts?" Harry said.

Carter raised his eyebrows. "You're really wallowing in the sports bar ambiance of this place."

Harry shrugged. "Yeah, so? I guess since you lost so badly at pool—"

"By one ball!" Carter said, then turned to Frank. "Right? Just one ball?"

Frank nodded but didn't look up from his phone. "Yep. One ball. Just like my cousin."

Carter exchanged a startled look with Harry before he turned back to Frank. "That was a lot of personal information about your cousin. Anything more to add to that proclamation?"

"No, not really." Frank looked up from his phone and

gestured toward the bar. "I think I'm going to go track down some of my friends."

Carter nodded. "Okay. Sure."

He watched Frank walk off through the crowd, his plastic wings brushing along people to either side of him. When Carter turned back to Harry, he noticed Brian had moved on as well.

"They both backed out?" Carter asked.

Harry shrugged. "Some people don't like darts. Sorry, looks like you lost out on some jostle and tussle from Frank." He raised his eyebrows. "Since we're standing here, how about those darts? Unless you're scared I'll beat you at them as well?"

"No," Carter said. "Lead the way."

Harry turned his back on Carter, but put both hands behind himself, wrists resting at the small of his back. He waggled his fingers and turned his head slightly to talk to Carter over his shoulder. "Grab hold and I'll tow you through the crowd."

"Like a water-skier?"

"Just like that," Harry said. "I can make a powerboat sound if you want."

"Seems like that should be some kind of kink."

Carter twined the fingers of both of his hands with Harry's, surprised at the softness of his skin. Harry moved through the crowd, his height and width easily forging a path. Carter kept his focus on Harry's back, watching the movement of his shoulders beneath the thin fabric of his T-shirt, and the way his hips shifted back and forth as he maneuvered around people. Earlier, he'd casually noticed the swell of Harry's ass, but until this moment, he hadn't seen Harry as anything more than a friend of Lizzie's who was challenged in both style and fashion. Now, holding onto Harry's hands just inches above the man's ass, he couldn't help but see him as a tall, strong man.

And he had no idea what to do with this sudden new perspective.

THE CUPID CRAWL

Harry stopped abruptly and Carter plowed into him, their hands becoming trapped between them. A woman who had been following behind Carter bumped into his back, pressing him even more firmly against Harry.

"Oh," Carter said, sandwiched between the woman behind him and Harry.

The bump from behind had forced their still-joined hands to slide down, and Harry's palm suddenly cupped Carter's crotch. Carter couldn't move, but he gasped when Harry's fingers momentarily tightened around his entire package: cock and balls.

Carter's first thought was Harry had gigantic hands. His second was how was he supposed to get his junk out of those massive hands? Followed quickly by another thought: was that what he really wanted?

Any need for Carter to act was taken away when Harry released Carter's hands and pulled his own around in front of him. He turned his head to look over his shoulder at Carter, cheeks practically crimson with a blush. Carter realized Harry was embarrassed by what had happened, and wondered why he didn't feel more embarrassed himself.

As a matter of fact, he was more than a little turned on.

"Sorry about that," Harry said. "I didn't mean to cop a feel. There's a bit of a traffic jam up here."

"It's okay," Carter said. "Not your fault. I got rear ended, so it pushed me into you."

Harry may have muttered something about Carter being rear ended before turning away, but Carter couldn't hear him over the music and the crowd. Carter might have started to see Harry in a different light, but that didn't mean Harry had come to the same conclusion about him.

Moments later, the jam up of people cleared out, and Harry led the way forward once again. This time, however, he didn't reach back for Carter's hands, instead letting him keep up on his own. They reached the electronic dart machine set in a corner near the front entrance, and Harry fished some quarters from his front pocket.

"Oh, we have to pay?" Carter asked. "Let me pay for darts since you must have paid for pool."

"And break my winning streak against you?" Harry grinned as he plugged quarters into the dart machine. "No way."

"That's how it's going to be, huh?" Carter said.

Harry finished feeding quarters into the machine and turned to face him. He bent down low and put his face close alongside Carter's so he could whisper in his ear. "Oh yeah, Carter Walsh, this is how it's going to be."

A shiver rattled down Carter's back, which he attributed to his proximity to the front entrance. Never mind that the door was shut tight, and he didn't feel a draft.

Harry seemed to have gotten over his embarrassment at accidentally grabbing Carter's crotch since he soundly bested Carter in their first game of darts. Carter demanded a second game, and they jokingly insulted each other's techniques until Carter managed to best Harry.

"Two out of three?" Harry asked.

Carter raised his eyebrows. "If you want to lose by two games, sure."

"Someone's feeling their oats," Harry said.

"Showing your age with that saying," Carter said.

"Showing yours by knowing what it means."

On and on it continued, until they both had only bull's-eyes left to win the third game. After several rounds with no luck, Carter managed to calm his racing heart and mind and hit the center bullseye, winning the game.

"Nice shot," Harry said, and held his hand up.

Carter gave him a high five just as Vic got on the PA system to draw the next winner.

"Remember, folks, the prizes get better and better as the day goes on," Vic said. "So it's definitely worth it to hit every bar on the crawl."

The prize this time were tickets to a Boston Bruins game, and a woman held the winning ticket. She and her girlfriend were excited to have the tickets, shouting "Charlie!" at each other as they held hands and jumped up and down.

"Is Charlie one of the players or something?" Carter asked.

Harry tapped on his phone a moment, and then turned it to show Carter a shirtless picture of a hot young man with a ripped torso and sexy smile.

"Charlie Coyle," Harry said. "Number thirteen on the Boston Bruins."

"I'm starting to see the appeal in hockey," Carter said.

"I thought you might."

Vic was back on the microphone. "We're halfway through the Cupid Crawl now. Is everyone having a good time?"

A roar of approval went up from the attendees.

"Excellent. Who knows the name of the next bar?"

There was some chatter in the crowd, and then a man shouted, "Hommes, bitches!"

"Right!" Vic said. "It's a sleek and stylish gay bar. We'll be boarding the shuttles in about ten minutes, so finish your drinks, hit the restrooms, and meet me at the door to find out what shuttle you're on."

The crowd moved toward the back of the bar where the restrooms were located. Carter and Harry exchanged a look.

"No restroom for you?" Harry asked.

Carter shook his head. "I'm good. You?"

"Same here. Need a quick drink before we get on the shuttle?"

"I'm okay, thanks."

Harry smiled and nodded. "You're more than okay, Carter. I hope you know that."

"What?" Carter blushed, and a warm feeling of satisfaction coursed through him. Both reactions were quite surprising. "Well, thanks. That's really nice."

He should have left it at that. It had been a nice compliment, and Carter had thanked Harry appropriately. But, of course, his defensive sassiness kicked in, and Carter had to follow what he'd said up with, "I guess my trouncing you at darts took some of the steam out of your engine."

He immediately regretted saying it. There had been no reason for him to tack on a sassy dig after his thank you. Why had he done that?

Because he'd realized he had started to like Harry. Or, rather, Carter had started to like Harry more than he'd ever expected to like a man who looked like Harry. And in a different way than he liked the guys he met on Grindr or in the bars. And that scared him. A lot.

Harry, arms crossed and a somewhat smug smirk on his face, looked at him. Just stood and looked at him. Carter fidgeted and was about to ask him what his deal was when Harry leaned in closer and said, "I see you, Carter Walsh."

Carter snorted and furrowed his brow. "I hope so. I'm standing right in front of you. Oh, is that why I beat you at darts? Are these not your dart playing glasses?"

"Nope. But I want you to know that I see you, Carter. Very well. And I like what I see." Harry straightened up and tipped his head toward the restroom area. "I'm going to hit the restroom before we get on that shuttle and the driver hits every pothole on the way to the next bar."

Carter's head was spinning like he'd just stepped off a carnival ride. He didn't need to say anything in response to Harry's statement. All he needed to do was laugh to show he had heard and understood what Harry had said. But his snarky side couldn't keep quiet for long, especially after Harry had told him he 'saw him very well.'

So, before he realized it, he said, "Good idea, you're older and your bladder control is probably slipping a bit now anyway."

Harry chuckled, shook his head, and turned away. He looked once over his shoulder at Carter, then followed the crowd toward the bathroom.

Carter groaned and put his face in his hands. What the hell was wrong with him? Harry obviously liked him, right? But Harry was so different from the guys Carter usually went for, he didn't think about Harry that way. Did he?

No, Harry liking him was ridiculous. Maybe they'd been getting along during pool and darts, but there wasn't anything more to it. Harry had been making the rounds during the Cupid Crawl, like Carter had himself. Only Harry, being pansexual, had a lot more options than Carter.

And Harry hadn't hooked up with anyone in a bathroom stall. At least, not that Carter knew about.

Plus Harry was friends with Lizzie, and, yikes, he didn't want to get anywhere near that train wreck again. There was no way Carter could find himself liking Harry, and Harry most likely didn't feel that way about Carter. It was all just some kind of misunderstanding. It was loud in the bar, and they'd both been drinking.

The crowd parted as if by magic, giving Carter a direct sightline on Harry's backside where he stood in line outside the men's room. The T-shirt stretched tight across his shoulders, and his ass looked great in his stone-washed jeans. Carter's stomach flipped as his heart pounded.

He'd checked Harry out. Again. And much more thoroughly this time. He hadn't simply been checking Harry out, he'd been cruising him. Not only that, he was suddenly aware that he was hoping he and Harry were assigned to the same shuttle. That would be easy to make happen, all he'd need to do was talk with Vic and he'd put them together.

But doing that would be manipulating whatever passed for happenstance and coincidence. And it would mean admitting that something more than a passing attraction to Harry might be simmering inside him.

"You're totally staring at Harry's ass."

Carter started and spun around. Ivy stood behind him, sipping from her flask as she eyed him shrewdly.

"No I wasn't."

"Yes you were."

"No, I wasn't."

"Yes, you were." She took another swig from the flask and offered it to him.

"No thanks."

"You won't drink from my flask, but you'll blow a stranger in a bathroom stall?" Ivy shrugged and tucked the flask in an inner pocket of her velvet jacket. "I see you have priorities."

"Look, I don't owe you or anybody else here an explanation for how I live my life or whose ass I might have been staring at."

"Whose ass was it?"

Carter turned again to find Harry standing right behind him, eyebrows raised as he waited for a response.

"Uh, what's that?" Carter managed to say though his tongue felt too big for his mouth. Why was he acting this way around Harry?

"Whose ass were you staring at?" Harry cast his gaze around them before looking back at Carter. "Would I like him?"

"Uhh..." Carter's brain shut down, and he seemed to have forgotten how to form spoken words.

"That guy with the tight red shorts," Ivy said. "The one who played pool with you guys."

"Frank?" Harry said.

"Frank?" Ivy said. "That's his name? Frank? What the hell is up with your names? It's like you were all born in the 1940s or something." With a disgusted sound, Ivy stomped off, the breadth of her wingspan sending people scurrying out of her way.

"She's an interesting character," Harry said, looking after her. "I like her." He turned back to Carter. "Do you?"

"Like her? Yeah, sure. She's a riot." He gestured toward the rest rooms. "You know, I do think I'm going to make a pit stop before we get on the shuttles."

"Oh. Okay. Sure. I'll just... I'll just go get my shuttle assignment. If we're not on the same shuttle, I guess I'll see you at the next bar."

"Yeah, I'll see you there."

Carter walked away from Harry and forced himself not to look back. He'd just met the guy, there was no reason for him to feel this way. He wasn't an insta-love kind of guy. There might be a flash fire of lustful attraction, but nothing deep enough to make him start acting like a middle school kid who wanted to sit next to his crush on the bus. He was too old to be acting this way.

At the next bar, he was going to play it cool. Really cool. He was going to be so cool he'd be ice cold.

CHAPTER NINE

Carter didn't see Harry on his assigned shuttle, which made him a little sad, at first, before he reminded himself he was going to be ice cold. Unfortunately, Aaron-who-doesn't-use-Grindr and his buddies, including Versatile Joe, were on the same shuttle, and Carter dropped into the first available seat he came to, trying to stay as far from them as possible.

An attractive man sat beside him, wearing a red baseball hat with the words Make America Love Again printed on the front. He introduced himself as John, and asked if Carter liked his hat.

"To be honest, it's a little off-putting at first," Carter said. "I think there's a gut reaction to hats like that now, even if they do have a positive message."

"Sure, sure," John said with a shrug. "But wouldn't it be great if people didn't automatically fear a red hat?"

"I'm not sure fear is the emotion that's triggered," Carter said. "I think anger would be more correct."

"Interesting," John said. "So you're not happy with the uptick in our economy?"

Carter wrinkled his nose and looked out the window. At that

moment, he wondered if being on the shuttle with someone like Lizzie would be any worse. He'd even deal with her sing/shouting "100 Bottles of Beer" and trying to get the rest of the shuttle to join in.

"How about we talk about something other than politics?" Carter suggested.

"You don't have an opinion on politics?" John asked.

"It's not that I don't have one," Carter said. "It's just that today's more for fun and meeting new people."

"We're meeting, and I'm a new person to you," John said.

Carter managed a tight smile. "Yes, that's true."

"The stock market's at an all-time high and there are hundreds of thousands of more jobs available," John went on.

"Yeah, but most people need two or three of them to make ends meet," Carter said.

John blinked then frowned. "That's not true."

Carter fixed him with a steely look. "Yeah, John, it is. A lot of this 'uptick' has been for the top one percent, leaving the rest of the country with the fizzle and smoke. And I haven't even touched on how they're chipping away at LGBT rights. So, yeah, I'm glad you've changed the wording on your hat to something much more palatable. And, also yeah, that was total sarcasm."

As if he'd timed it, the shuttle pulled up in front of the next stop, a gay bar called Hommes, and Carter stood.

"Excuse me."

John slid his legs to the side to allow him past. Carter followed a group of Crawlers off the shuttle and into the bar. His heart pounded and his face felt flushed, and he realized with surprise that he'd clenched his fists.

He strode to the restroom, and as he pushed through the door, nearly ran into VersatileJoe75.

"Sorry," Joe said, then recognized Carter. "Oh, hi."

"You don't have to talk with me," Carter said. "It's all right."

Joe shrugged. "Okay."

Joe left the bathroom and Carter entered a stall, closing the door and leaning against it with his head on his forearm. What the hell had been that guy John's deal? Carter had thought John had sat beside him to get to know him, maybe flirt a little. But then he'd gone off about politics, and damn if Carter was going to sit there and just nod in agreement.

"Hello?"

Carter lifted his head off his arm and frowned. What now?

"Occupied," Carter said.

"So, hey, Carter, it's John. From the shuttle?"

"Oh. Hi."

"Look, I didn't mean to piss you off," John said. "I'm not even really into politics, to be honest. I just wore the hat as a joke, you know?"

Carter rolled his eyes. "Yeah? And how's that joke been going over with people so far?"

"About as well as you'd expect." John sighed. "Look, can I buy you a drink or something?"

Carter was glad John couldn't see the face he made. But, he'd joined the Cupid Crawl to meet new people. Besides, one drink wouldn't hurt.

And, a quiet voice whispered in the back of his mind, *you can hang out at the bar and watch for Harry to arrive.*

No, that was definitely not the reason. He was just going to be open minded about John and his goddamn hat.

"Yeah, sure," Carter said. "Give me a couple of minutes and I'll meet you at the bar."

"Oh, sorry," John said. "Are you... I didn't mean to interrupt you.... In there."

"I'm not taking a crap," Carter grumbled. "I'm taking a moment."

A new voice chimed in, loud and belligerent with a bit of slur to the words.

"Take your moment somewhere else. Some of us really do have to shit."

Carter sighed and opened the stall door. Five men turned to look at him, and he saw John standing by the exit, still wearing his fucking hat. John shrugged, mouthed the word "Sorry," then mimed drinking and pointed toward the door before leaving the restroom.

A man with an expression of intense concentration brushed past Carter to enter the stall, slamming the door behind him. Carter avoided looking at everyone else as he washed his hands. He grabbed some paper towel and fled the bathroom, relieved no one had tried to talk with him.

He decided he was pretty much done with the Cupid Crawl. He had more than half a mind to walk right out the door of the bar and get a Lyft to take him home. But, Vic had said there were bigger and better prizes the longer the night went on.

And, the quiet voice whispered, *you would miss out on getting to know Harry a bit better.*

Carter shook his head as he forged a path through the crowd in the opposite direction of the bar. That was not even a consideration for his continued attendance at the Cupid Crawl. Harry was so not his type. Like at all.

But, the voice argued, *like Will would most likely say if he were there, that might be a good thing.*

Carter made a slow circuit of the place. It had been at least a year since he'd been to Hommes, and he was glad to see the owner had made some updates. A wall had been knocked out, opening up the bar area to the dance floor, and the deejay booth had been raised. Several couples were dancing to a high energy song Carter didn't recognize. Was it some recent hit, or an older song remixed until it was practically unrecognizable? Was he that out of touch with the latest dance music? Hooking up in his apartment via Grindr may have kept him out of touch with the latest music.

He took another lap of the place. Rather than calming him down, it left him a bit more on edge. He felt irked, and didn't really know why.

The quiet voice inside him knew why he felt this way, but Carter refused to listen to it. That quiet voice could totally fuck off. He needed to stop hearing that goddamn voice, so he stopped at an empty two-high table near a set of speakers, letting the music thump every thought out of his head as he totally and completely didn't think about Harry.

He was not at all edgy because he had yet to catch sight of Harry. There was no way he was that invested in someone who, by all rights, he shouldn't even be attracted to.

Good God, had he even thought that? He wasn't attracted to Harry. The man had been friendly and outgoing, and Carter had enjoyed talking with him while they'd played pool and darts. That was all. There was not one whit of attraction at all. Not even a little bit. There was no urge to see Harry peel off that ridiculous T-shirt with the graphic of Cupid's abs, or see him push those stone-washed jeans down and step out of them.

Harry was definitely a briefs man. Carter could tell just by looking at him. White cotton briefs he most likely bought in a package of six from someplace like Target or Walmart.

Damn, though, Carter would like to see how he filled out those briefs. His ass did look good in those jeans.

Oh, for fuck's sake. What the hell was wrong with him?

"Want to dance?"

Carter turned, the bright smile fading as he found it wasn't Harry who had asked him to dance. It was a guy he hadn't met yet, attractive, with dark hair, blue eyes, and a scruff of beard. He also looked a little nervous, which played to Carter's sympathies.

"Hi," Carter said. "Sure, yeah. A dance would be good."

With a final scan of the bar—absolutely not looking for Harry, no way—he followed the guy out to the dance floor.

The stranger turned out to be a good dancer, and fun too. But Carter's eyes seemed to have minds of their own, and he kept looking toward the bar area every few minutes. Another shuttle must have arrived because a rush of familiar faces came through the door, just not the one he wouldn't admit he was searching for.

"Looking for someone?" Carter's dance partner asked.

His proximity and voice made Carter jump. He laughed with embarrassment and stepped in closer to the man to speak into his ear. "Sort of. I was talking with a guy at the last bar—"

"You played pool and darts with him," the man said. "Looked like you were really hitting it off."

"Oh?"

Carter stepped back and frowned. Had this guy been following him through each of the previous bars?

"I'm not a stalker," the guy said. "I just saw you at the first bar and thought you were cute. I've been looking for an opportunity to talk to you." He extended a hand. "I'm Rob."

"Carter."

He shook Rob's hand and they continued dancing. The song changed and Carter wasn't really feeling the new music. Rob seemed to be lost in the song, however, so Carter went through the motions, entertaining himself by thinking about hanging out with Harry at Hip Check. It had been easy to talk with Harry, and Harry had kept up with Carter's snark and jokes.

The memory of Harry accidentally cupping his crotch roared into his mind and sent a rush of lust burning through him. He wished now that Harry had kept his hand there a little longer. Or, maybe, a lot longer.

"Want a drink?"

Rob had leaned in close in order to be heard above the music, and it made Carter jump again.

"Sorry, I was lost in the music," Carter lied. "A drink would be nice."

He followed Rob to the bar. A few feet away, John leaned on the bar with a drink in front of him, his red Make America Love Again hat still planted firmly on his head. John stared cold-eyed at him and Carter stared right back before he turned to Rob. He asked for a bottled beer, and once Rob handed it to him, Carter followed Rob to a four high table just abandoned by a group of people.

"So tell me about yourself," Rob said.

"Not much to tell," Carter said and took a long pull off his beer.

"Well, what brought you out to the Cupid Crawl?" Rob asked, and Carter had to give him points for tenacity. "Did that friend I saw you hanging out with at the last bar talk you into it?"

"What? Oh, no. Someone I work with told me about the Cupid Crawl, and I decided at the last minute to check it out." Carter gulped his beer. "I just met Harry today."

"Harry's the guy you were playing pool and darts with?"

"Yeah."

"You two looked like you really got along," Rob said. "Laughing and joking. I thought you'd known each other a long time." He held his hands up as if he were surrendering. "Again, I'm not a stalker."

Carter shrugged. "I met him today, and I guess we hit it off. But we were just having fun."

Carter's mind didn't seem to agree with his statement because it flashed back to Harry's unintentional grope, reviving the memory of the rush Carter felt, and how that quick touch had seemed more intimate than the majority of any sex act he'd engaged in with his Grindr dates. And hot on the heels of that memory came the words Harry had said to him: *I want you to know that I see you, Carter. Very well. And I like what I see.*

What the hell was he supposed to do about a guy who said stuff like that? Especially on a first by-chance meeting?

"If you say so," Rob said.

Carter frowned. "What's that mean?"

"Maybe you were too caught up in the games, but I saw the way he watched you," Rob said. "He's really into.... you."

"Harry?" Carter's voice went up at least an octave. "That Harry? With the mustache and the center part in his hair and the T-shirt with the cartoon Cupid abs on it? No. That's not... No, we aren't really compatible."

"Well, you might want to tell him that," Rob said. "Because from where I was standing, he was pretty much eye-fucking you the entire time."

I want you to know that I see you, Carter. Very well. And I like what I see.

Carter looked away, his thoughts dancing, spinning, ricocheting off each other. Harry's words echoed around his brain, making him feel warm and nervous and terrified. Who said that when they first met someone? No sane person, that's who. Maybe that explained Harry's actions all day that day: he was crazy.

Only, deep down, Carter didn't want Harry to be crazy. No, he wanted Harry to be honest and open and patient and interested in Carter in a way no one else had been in a very long time, if ever.

But that wasn't something that could just happen in a day. And what the hell did his brain think his cock wanted from good old Harry? Better, yet, what did his brain think his heart wanted?

And what the fuck was wrong with him, thinking about his heart and what it wanted from Harry? This wasn't like him, not at all. Maybe he'd had too much to drink, and the whole "love is in the air" vibe of the Cupid Crawl had infected him.

But Harry had told him he "saw" Carter, and he liked what he'd seen.

What the hell was he supposed to do with that?

Carter had felt a small spark in his chest when he'd taken Harry's hands, but he could have just been imagining things. Again, it was very possible he'd been infected by all the Cupids and heart-shaped arrows on display.

But Carter couldn't deny that spark had ignited into something bigger and hotter when Harry had inadvertently fondled him not long after.

The front entrance of the bar opened, and a burst of cold air rushed in, causing Carter to shiver and look in that direction. Harry walked in, blinking as his eyes adjusted to the bar's dim lighting and hair mussed up from the wind. Of Lizzie there was no sign, and Carter wondered if she had passed out and Harry had simply left her on the shuttle.

On second thought, Harry didn't seem the type to do something like that.

"Speak of the devil," Rob said.

"Yeah, devil may be right," Carter said, and turned away before he made eye contact with Harry. He needed some time to think about everything.

"You're really not into him?" Rob asked.

"Not a bit," Carter said. "Why? Are you interested in him?"

Rob lifted a shoulder in a half-shrug and looked past Carter to Harry. "He's big and masculine and looks like he could flip me around in bed without breaking a sweat. And the way I caught him looking at you makes me think he's pretty passionate. That translates to one hot daddy fuck."

Carter managed not to look over his shoulder. But the way Rob described Harry made Carter's stomach tighten and his cock stir with interest. The urge to look at Harry was strong, so to keep from doing it he drank some more of his beer. The memory of Harry grabbing him popped up, and he squashed it down, only to have it pop back up again.

He'd just met Harry, he shouldn't be so interested so fast. Also, Harry was saddled with Lizzie, and Carter could definitely avoid all doses of that much toxicity.

I want you to know that I see you, Carter. Very well. And I like what I see.

"He's on the prowl," Rob said, his eyes moving as he apparently watched Harry cross the bar.

"You seem really interested in him," Carter said. "Why don't you go up and talk to him?"

Rob studied him a moment. "You wouldn't care?"

"Harry and I just met today," Carter said. "I have no claim on him."

"If you're sure you don't mind, I might go over and introduce myself."

"Sure, go ahead."

Rob sat for a moment, staring off to Carter's left, apparently at Harry. Finally, with a nod, he slid off the stool. "I'm going to do it. I'm going to talk to him."

Carter lifted his beer bottle. "Good luck."

He watched over his shoulder as Rob approached Harry, who was talking to someone out of Carter's line of sight. Harry shifted position, allowing Carter to see that it was Vic he was talking to. Rob stood just behind Harry, maybe waiting for a break in their conversation. But from Harry's expression, it looked like his discussion with Vic was pretty serious. Carter wondered if it had to do with Lizzie, then was surprised by a small wave of sympathy for her. What the hell was going on with him today? Attraction to Harry and sympathy for Dizzy Frizzy Lizzie? It had to be the End Times.

Harry turned, saw Rob standing close behind him, and managed a tight smile. Rob said something and Harry leaned in to hear better. After Rob spoke again, Harry smiled and squeezed Rob's shoulder.

Carter was surprised at a quiet surge of emotion upon witnessing the gesture. Was it jealousy? Or envy? Maybe a touch of both? He couldn't be certain what it was, but he sure as hell didn't think he knew Harry well enough at all to be experiencing either of those emotions. Did he?

∽

CARTER SAT at the two high, swinging his feet like a little kid as he looked around. A sad and quiet sense of loss welled inside him. He felt disconnected from everyone around him, and suddenly understood all too well that old cliché about standing in a crowded room and feeling completely alone. Without a friend to hang with, Carter didn't know what to do with himself.

When he'd been in his early twenties, he'd never had a problem going to bars alone. He'd talked with complete strangers, danced to nearly every song, and more often than not, left the bar with a few phone numbers or IM profiles. But now that he was closing in on thirty, Carter had come to realize he didn't enjoy going out on his own. He really missed Will, more than he'd thought he would. They were the perfect wingmen: able to make each other laugh about the guys who were out of reach, and prime each other's egos before approaching someone. If Will was there with him, Carter would have someone to talk with about his confusing feelings for Harry. And so sitting there, alone, in the middle of the Cupid Crawl, Carter realized Valentine's Day wasn't the same without Will.

He might as well get used to it though. Now that Will was married, from here on out, all of his Valentine's Days were going to be booked up. And Will most likely wouldn't want to hang out at bars very much anymore either, not with someone as hot as Rex waiting at home for him. Sure there might be some weekends Will would be free when Rex would be on the road performing, but

Carter could practically predict Will's desire to stay home on the weekends.

Maybe Carter and Will could start getting together more outside of bars. Play video games or watch movies or learn to cook together. With a start, Carter realized those things he'd been imagining were usually activities couples would do together. And he and Will were not a couple in that sense of the word. So, while it would have been nice to spend more quality time with his best friend, Carter didn't see how doing that would help him find someone special for himself.

Someone came up beside him and he found Ivy standing beside him, flask in hand.

"I'm beginning to think you really are an Angel of Death, the way you just sort of show up," Carter said.

Ivy grinned. "Nervous?"

"No," Carter said, then shrugged. "A little, maybe."

"Anyone here you fancy?" Ivy asked.

Carter's thoughts went immediately to Harry, but he kept his expression neutral as he said, "There are some attractive people here. I'm still on the fence about some. How about you? Find anyone to juxtapose with your darkness?"

Ivy sneered. "My darkness is just fine on its own. All I've seen here are guys who spend too much time at the gym or not enough time, and girls with too much hair or five heads."

"Five heads?" Carter asked with a laugh. "You've seen women here who have five heads?"

"Not five separate heads, you weirdo," Ivy said with a shake of her head. "But a really high hairline, so instead of having a forehead, they have a five-head."

Carter smiled and stared at her. "That's... oddly specific, and fitting in some cases."

"Right?" Ivy returned his smile. "You will think of that for the rest of your life now. You're welcome."

A new voice said, "Hey there."

Carter looked to his left and found a handsome man smiling at him. The new arrival's bare torso rippled with muscles, and a heart pierced with a number of arrows had been tattooed on his left pectoral.

"Hi," Carter said, and gestured to the man's chest as his brain automatically clicked into flirt mode. "Nice tat."

"Thanks."

"Any significance to the number of arrows in your heart?"

"Every boy I've loved and lost," the man said. "I'm Steve."

"Carter."

Steve's smile widened. "Carter the Farter?"

Ivy laughed and immediately walked away.

"Oh for fuck's... Nice to meet you, bye." Carter slid off the stool and walked off in a different direction from Ivy.

Fucking Dizzy Frizzy Lizzie and her big mouth. What the actual fuck was wrong with her? And to think he'd felt a tiny bit of sympathy for her just a few minutes ago. Yeah, this whole Stupid Crawl thing had been a bad idea. He needed to abandon ship before it got even worse. He'd made it to bar number four; he could consider that a success.

Carter headed for the bar's main door, turning this way and that as he made his way through the crowd. When he was a few yards from the exit, a large man stepped in front of him. Daylight coming in through the open door cast the man in silhouette, and for a split second Carter thought it was Harry. A small and confusing jolt of happiness zipped through him, until he realized it wasn't Harry after all, but rather Vic.

"Hold up there, Carter," Vic said. "We're not boarding the shuttles for another ten minutes."

"Yeah, about that," Carter said. "I'm pretty much done with the Cupid Crawl. Thanks for a fun time, but I'm ready to check out."

Vic pursed his lips and nodded. "I see, I see. You're free to do that, of course."

"That's kind of you."

"But, I will say that you would be missed."

Carter snorted a sarcastic laugh. "Oh really. By who?"

"Whom," Vic said.

Carter glared. "Fine, grammar Nazi. By whom?"

"Well, Harry for one."

"Harry?" Carter turned and waved a hand to the spot where Harry and Rob stood talking. "You mean that Harry? The one talking to the hot guy?"

"Yeah, that Harry. The one who hasn't been able to focus on the conversation he's having with that hot guy because he keeps looking over here at you."

Carter turned back to Vic. "What?"

Vic nodded. "Harry has been looking for you since he arrived. He made sure Lizzie was hanging with a group of girls who said they'd keep an eye on her, and then he started looking for you. He came up to me and was asking about you when that hot guy approached him."

"Oh."

Carter didn't know what he was more surprised about, the fact that Lizzie was apparently still able to walk, or that Harry had been looking for him. He brushed a hand down the front of his shirt to smooth out the wrinkles and pulled his shoulders back.

"Two more bars after this one?" Carter asked.

"Two more," Vic said. "Think you can manage to have a good time?"

Carter shrugged. "I'll try. But the final two bars are going to figure prominently in my Yelp! Review of this thing."

Vic laughed. "Noted. I'm about to do the fourth giveaway, and you don't want to miss it. Plus the final prize is a pretty big one. I think you might like it."

"You keep saying that," Carter said. "Shouldn't the Cupid Crawl be entertaining enough without you having to bribe people to attend and stick it out through all six bars?"

"It helps get people to sign up. And, besides, everyone loves to win a prize." Vic smiled and squeezed Carter's upper arm. "I'm going to get on the mic and do the next drawing. Keep your ticket handy."

"Oh, it's handy."

Vic walked off and Carter pulled the ticket from his pocket. Harry and Rob had moved away from the bar and out of sight, and Carter tried not to think about it too much.

The music volume lowered and Vic got on the microphone to address the crowd.

"Hey Crawlers! Time for another prize drawing, so reach deep into your pockets and dig out those tickets. This prize is a champagne breakfast for six at Drag Queen Bingo. This is a great prize pack that includes food, drinks, and bingo cards, not to mention a meet and greet afterwards with the queens. Now check your tickets and get ready."

Vic reached into the manila envelope and pulled out a ticket stub. He read the number and a guy a few feet away from Carter gave a shout of glee. Carter smiled as he watched the man claim his prize and his group of friends cheered him on. He looked around for Harry but didn't see him, though he did catch a glimpse of Lizzie through the crowd, and quickly stepped out of sight behind a group of women.

"Almost time to board the shuttles for bar number five," Vic said into the mic. "Who knows what bar is next?"

"Minor Chords!" someone shouted.

"Right," Vic said. "It's a dueling piano bar. So load up your Cupid wings and bows and arrows, hit the bathrooms, then see me for shuttle assignments."

Carter had lost track of Harry, but with a decisive nod, he

promised himself to spend some more time with the man at the next bar. If Vic was right about the way Harry had had been watching him, Carter should give Harry more of a chance. And if nothing came of it, so be it. But the least he could do was keep an open mind.

Feeling a bit more hopeful, he turned toward the exit. A thought, however, stopped him in his tracks. He hadn't witnessed Harry's reactions himself. Well, not to the extent Vic had described them. What if Vic had seen Carter and Harry together and was lying about Harry watching him? What if all of it was just some crazy plot Vic had come up with to keep Carter on the Crawl?

But for what reason? The Cupid Crawl wasn't hurting for attendees, that much was clear. So why would Vic do something like that?

Well, why would anyone lie about anything? Maybe he got off on it, like a weird power trip. Or he just liked to mess with people.

"You ready to get on the shuttle, Carter?" Vic came up behind him, clipboard at the ready.

Carter nodded as he gave him a long, steady look. "Sure."

"Go ahead and get on shuttle three," Vic said, then tipped him a wink. "Same one Harry's on."

"Oh, thanks," Carter said. He hesitated, then took a step closer to Vic and said, "Hey, about what you said earlier…"

"Vic! We need our shuttle!"

A man came up behind Vic and grabbed him in a bear hug. More people surrounded them, and Carter moved back as Vic laughed and read shuttle assignments off his clipboard.

With a final glance around the bar—still no sign of Harry— Carter decided he'd better use the restroom first. By the time he boarded the shuttle, he saw Harry sitting toward the back and they exchanged smiles.

And right next to Harry sat Rob.

Carter's stomach tightened and his heart seemed to drop a few inches inside his chest, as if whatever had been propping it up all the years of his life had suddenly given way.

Lizzie sat in the row behind Harry, but thankfully hadn't seen him. Carter quickly claimed a window seat near the front of the shuttle. Not long after he'd sat down, a young woman sat beside him. Without so much as a glance in his direction, she turned her back to him in order to talk with her friends sitting across the aisle. It had been a long time since Carter had felt so dismissed, so he occupied himself by looking through Grindr, all the while assuring himself that everything was going to work out in the end.

Work out for who, though, was the big question. Rob, maybe? Harry? Or Carter himself?

Minor Chords, the next bar on the Cupid Crawl, would be better; he could feel it.

CHAPTER TEN

Minor Chords was a complete shit show.

The bar was small and already crowded by the time the Cupid Crawl attendees arrived. It was a long, narrow space, with the bar running along one side and the dueling pianos arranged facing each other on a stage at the far end. When Carter entered the place, the piano players, a man and a woman, were just finishing a somber version of "Walking On Sunshine," that did nothing to boost his mood. Minor Chords seemed a more than apt name for the place if that's what they had to look forward to.

There were no available tables and very little standing room, so the Cupid Crawlers stood in clumps, angel wings poking and jabbing. Those who were lightly dressed or shirtless shivered every time the door opened. The volume on the pianos—keyboards set inside grand piano-like structures—had been cranked up, so there was very little to be had in the way of conversation. Carter caught a glimpse of Ivy standing near the entrance, black feathers in her large wings trembling in the wind every time the door opened. He let his gaze move slowly over the crowd until he spotted Harry standing a few people away, looking very uncomfortable with his elbows tucked in tight to avoid injuring the Crawler to either side.

As the pianists launched into a minor chord version of Britney Spears's "Toxic," someone bumped gently against Carter's right arm. He was surprised to discover Harry had shifted places with some people and now stood beside him.

Leaning down, Harry spoke/shouted into Carter's ear. "Too bad there's no dance floor."

Carter laughed and gestured for Harry to lean down so he could speak/shout into his ear.

"Used to be, but people kept curling up in the fetal position and sobbing from the music, so they did away with it."

Harry laughed and nodded before straightening up to his full height once again.

Vic seemed to realize pretty quickly that Minor Chords wasn't going to work out for their group. He started making his way through the tightly packed groups of Crawlers, telling everyone to finish their drink and go back out to the shuttles.

"We'll do the last two drawings at the next bar," Vic said into Carter's ear. "Just get on a shuttle where there's room."

Carter lost track of Harry and Ivy in the rush of Crawlers escaping from the dirge of popular music. He saw them sitting in different spots on one of the shuttles, but realized there were no seats left, so he climbed onto a different one. A young guy with glassy eyes and an unsteady walk dropped into the seat beside him.

"Hey," the guy said, sending a fog of beer-breath rolling over Carter.

"Oh, wow," Carter gasped and held a hand up to his mouth to catch a fresh breath. "Um, hey."

"Drake." The guy stuck out a big hand, and Carter shook it.

"Carter."

Drake grinned. "Hey, you're the Farter?"

THE RIDE to the final bar—a gay and lesbian dance bar called Cheeky Monkey—was the longest of Carter's life. Longer than any family road trip he'd had to endure, sandwiched between his brother and sister in the backseat. Longer even than his final driving test when he'd been sixteen and sweating through his shirt.

Drake asked him countless questions about the nickname Lizzie had given him and, apparently, told to every person on the Cupid Crawl. Carter dodged as many of the questions as he could, providing scant details or humorous antidotes to try and derail Drake. But the man was fart-focused, and by the time they'd reached the parking lot of Cheeky Monkey, Carter had told him the real story and Drake looked more than a little let down.

"That's it?" Drake said, brow furrowed. "You just let one slip when you thought you were alone?"

"That's it," Carter said with a shrug.

"Well fuck, that's nothing." Drake screwed up his face, lifted one butt cheek off the seat, and ripped loose a fart. "Everybody does that."

As if the stink of Drake's breath wasn't bad enough, now a noxious cloud of gas enveloped them. Without a word, Carter got to his feet and slid past Drake, making his way to the front of the shuttle. The minute the door opened, he stepped off and practically fled to the bar. He bypassed the bar made of glass block, skirted the hardwood dance floor already crowded with people moving to something upbeat and energetic and not some kind of pop music funeral dirge—thank God—and ducked into the men's bathroom. Entering a stall, he closed and locked the door behind him, and put his face in his hands.

What. The. Fucking. Hell.

This day. This crazy fucking day.

A rush of guys entered the bathroom, talking and laughing as they headed for the urinals and other open stalls. Carter stayed where he was, taking deep breaths to try and relax a bit as he also tried to convince himself parts of this day were a dream, just a bad, awful dream.

If one more fucking person he'd never met before called him Farter, he was going to lose it. And he was going to make sure Lizzie got a big dose of wrath before the day was over.

There were a couple of guys talking by the sink, but other than that, it seemed like the initial rush had subsided. He opened the stall door and stepped out in time to see Rob and Harry standing by the far sink.

Kissing.

Harry's hands were on Rob's chest, and Rob had his arms around Harry's neck.

Like an elevator with a snapped cable, Carter's heart plummeted. No emergency brakes, no air bag, just a free-fall into nothingness. The door opened and two guys walked in. Carter saw his chance and slipped out the door as the new arrivals cat-called to Harry and Rob. He didn't think Harry had seen him, however, and for that he really was grateful.

This crazy fucking day just became a hellaciously atrocious crazy fucking day.

So much for Harry watching him as he'd been talking to Rob. Vic had either lied about it, or had no idea what he was talking about.

So much for Harry "seeing" him, and liking what he saw.

So much for anything good happening on this bar crawl through Hell.

Carter made his way through the crowd, his thoughts pinging around like his brain was a bounce house in a wind storm. He didn't really know why he was so upset. Harry hadn't made him any promises, and Carter had no claims on him. After all, Carter had hooked up with VersatileJoe75 at the first bar, and that Hot Guy at the second one, so he really didn't have anything to be upset about.

Except for the fact that he did feel upset. And that annoyed him. No, more than annoyed him. It made him sad.

After his initial reaction to Harry, Carter had come to realize there was more to the man than what his appearance indicated. He could beat himself up all he wanted for being shallow and judging a book by its cover, and he deserved it. Carter had treated Harry badly at first, and so he deserved to be disappointed. He really needed to be happy for Harry, and hope things between him and Rob worked out for the best, even if it might only be for one day.

What made Carter think he and Harry could have something that would last longer than that? They didn't know anything about each other, so there was no reason for him to be thinking beyond a quick, and most likely hot, hook up.

And yet, Carter couldn't help wondering what Harry liked to do on the weekends. And which side of the bed he slept on, which brand of toothpaste he preferred, and what he did for fun, or to relax, or when he was bored.

Another upbeat song started, something Carter thought was vaguely familiar, but it might have been something brand new sampling something he knew. Either way, it was a distraction, and he was more than ready for it.

He headed to the dance floor and found an open spot in a back corner. At the moment, he wanted to dance by himself with no other thoughts or interruptions. Carter started moving to the song—definitely new and sampling something a few years old. It had been a long time since he'd been out dancing, and at first his movements were stiff. After a couple of minutes, however, he found the rhythm and closed his eyes, losing himself in the song.

After four songs, he'd danced hard enough to be coated in a

light sheen of sweat and felt a bit better. He decided he could use a drink, so he headed for the bar and ordered a bottle of water. His phone buzzed, making him jump, and he pulled it from his pocket to find a text message from Will.

No awards for Rex today. He's handling it better than I am.

Carter wrote back: *Boo about Rex being overlooked for awards. I bet you'll give him something to occupy his empty hands when you're back at your hotel.*

Moments later, Will's response arrived: *You're very dirty-minded, and quite correct. How's the bar crawl?*

Carter replied: *At the final bar. So far it's been a bust. I went off on a guy wearing a red hat and another guy farted to prove a point.*

Will's answer arrived quickly: *Can you FaceTime?*

Carter looked around. There was no good spot for a private video chat, and the music was pretty loud. He'd have to go outside again. Dammit, he really should have brought a coat.

He quickly wrote back to Will: *Give me a minute.*

Carter headed for the exit, gasping when he stepped outside as the cold air chilled his sweaty skin. He saw the shuttles lined up in the bar's parking lot and hurried over. The door on one of the shuttles was propped open, and Carter climbed onboard. There was no sign of the driver, so he took a seat near the back, out of the direct line of cold air coming in through the door, and opened the FaceTime app.

Will's face filled the screen of Carter's phone, and just the sight of his smile helped Carter relax a little bit.

"Hey, Cartier," Will said. "How are you?"

"I'm okay, Big Willie. Bummer that Rex didn't win."

"I think I'm more upset about it than he is," Will said, then looked around and held the phone closer to his face as he lowered his voice. "Although, to be fair, the guy who did win has a really amazing voice."

Carter feigned shock. "More amazing than your husband's?"

"I did not say those words," Will said. "I just said he has an amazing voice."

"Nice save."

"Rex's performance was awesome," Will said.

"Did he give a shout out to his one and only?" Carter held his phone closer and said, "And by that, I meant you."

"I know what you meant," Will said. "And, yes, he did give me a shout out at the end of the song."

"So sweet."

"I know. A guy could get a cavity just thinking about it."

"I've had quite a bit of dental work since you two got together," Carter said with an elaborate eye roll and heavy sigh.

"I'm sure it's not at all due to that grinding you do at night."

"You don't know that," Carter said.

"Oh, but I do," Will shot back. "We slept together a couple of weeks before deciding to be friends, remember?"

"No, I most certainly do not," Carter said, trying to act indignant.

"So tell me about your day. Some guy wore a red hat and another guy farted on you?

"Farted near me," Carter said. "To make a point that Lizzie blew the whole farting business way out of proportion."

"You've had a very full day."

"And to think I could have stayed home and done a Grindr sampler."

Will pouted. "Sorry it didn't go very well. How's Dizzy Frizzy Lizzie doing?"

"Oh, man, she is totally trashed."

"Really?"

"Really. If she doesn't puke in the bar, she's going to barf all over someone's backseat. I'm just glad she didn't puke in the shuttle on the way here."

"You're sitting in a shuttle right now?"

"The bar was too loud for a call, and the doors on this one were open." He looked around and made a face. "God, I hope nobody puked in here and they're airing it out."

"So gross. People are really getting into Valentine's Day, huh?"

"For sure."

"So, any hot prospects you're working on?" Will asked. "Meet anyone interesting in person?"

Carter shrugged. "A few. You know how I like to play the field."

"And by field you mean the Great Plains?" Will said with a chuckle.

"Ha ha."

Carter thought about Harry. He wondered if Harry had bought Rob a Crown and Seven and was exchanging flirty glances and suggestive comments. Or maybe Rob had convinced Harry to hit the dance floor, and Harry had his hands on Rob's hips, gripping him tight as he ground up against him. Carter wondered what it would have felt like to have Harry's hands gripping his hips, pulling him in close, maybe leaning down for a slow, sensual kiss.

Harry's kisses would definitely be slower and more sensual than anyone else's. Carter could tell that from their interactions so far.

"Hey, where'd you go?" Will asked.

"Sorry, what?" Carter realized his gaze had drifted off his phone, and he focused on it again.

"You had a strange expression for a few seconds there," Will said. "Like you were all dreamy about something, but also a little angry about it, too."

"Oh, you know how I am," Carter said and waved Will's concern away. "My moods pass like the clouds."

Will frowned. "You sure?"

"Of course I'm sure. You're not allowed to worry about me while you're off on vacation with your hot and talented husband. I'm out with people and enjoying myself. There's nothing for you to be concerned about."

"Okay," Will said, drawing the word out and not at all sounding convinced.

They chatted a bit more, then Rex appeared behind Will and shouted a greeting to Carter, who shouted one back. Before he disconnected, Will looked right into the camera of his phone and said, "You call me if you need to, okay?"

No use of the fun Cartier nickname, and no joking tone. The sincerity in Will's voice and expression tightened Carter's throat so much, all he could manage to respond with at first was a nod. He cleared his throat and was glad to hear his voice sounded steady when he said, "I will. You do the same."

"Love you, buddy," Will said.

"Love you, too. Now go be Rex's arm candy like a good trophy husband."

Will laughed and shook his head before saying, "Talk to you later."

"Threats now?" Carter smiled. "Take care. Go have fun."

The call ended and Carter looked out the window of the shuttle for a moment. He was chilled, but not enough to want to go back inside the bar. Instead, he opened Grindr and scrolled through the available profiles. No one caught his attention, so he closed the app and switched to Candy Crush.

Someone boarded the shuttle, and he looked up. His heart beat a little faster and a shiver went down his back when he saw Harry standing at the front of the shuttle staring at him.

"I've been looking for you," Harry said.

"Oh?" Carter's internal organs felt like they'd gotten all tangled up with each other, and his breath was coming in quick pants. He locked his phone and forced a smile, trying to sound aloof as he said, "Well, you found me. What's up?"

Harry made his way down the aisle and sat in the seat directly across. He kept his feet in the aisle and leaned forward, resting his wrists on his knees as he met Carter's gaze. Behind his glasses, Harry's blue eyes studied Carter's face. The close proximity allowed Carter to breathe in the clean tang of Harry's sweat, mixed with floral notes from his fabric softener, as well as a musky, woodsy smell that was most likely his deodorant.

"I thought you might have grabbed a ride home or something," Harry said.

"I considered it," Carter said. "But I didn't want to lose out on the grand prize drawing Vic's been talking up all day."

Harry smiled. "Do you know what it is?"

"Nope," Carter said. "But it's a grand prize, so it's got to be something good, right?"

"It's gotta be." Harry shifted position, moving closer to the edge of his seat and closing the distance between them. "I was worried I hadn't gotten a chance to say goodbye, and I didn't know how to get in touch with you."

"Oh?" Carter swallowed past a sudden lump in his throat. "Why would you need to get in touch with me?"

Harry inched closer. "To see if you might be open to helping me shop for clothes or something. You know, since you're so fancy and all."

Carter smiled, but his lips were so dry he was forced to lick them.

"I'd be willing to spread the gospel of fashion. But, couldn't Rob help you out with that?"

"Rob?" Harry frowned, then understanding hit and he ducked his head a moment before looking back at Carter, squinting through one eye. "Did you see the kiss in the bathroom?"

"Was there another one I may have missed?"

Harry's eyebrows went up. "Oh, my. Carter Walsh, if I didn't know any better, I'd say you sounded jealous."

"Well, then you don't any better," Carter said, and looked away.

Harry chuckled. "That kiss lasted maybe a few seconds, and I did not initiate it. He pretty much launched himself at me, and I had to push him back and tell him I wasn't interested."

Carter looked back. "Oh?"

"Yeah. And he got really embarrassed and ran off, and then, you know, I felt bad, so I had to go find him and apologize."

"And kiss him for real?" Carter said, hating the petulant snarkiness, and, yes, *jealousy*, he could hear in his tone.

"No, no more kisses. Not even a hug." Harry cleared his throat and said, "Now, about you helping me shop for clothes… Are you interested?"

"Well," Carter let out a heavy breath. "My services don't come cheap."

Harry moved closer still. By now his ass was half off the edge of the seat, and his left knee lightly touched the side of Carter's left knee. Even though he'd been with numerous men over the years, Carter had to admit that sitting there with Harry edging closer a little at a time was more sexually tense than anything he'd ever experienced before.

"Maybe we could work out some kind of, I don't know, payment plan or something?"

Closer still, and now Harry's face was inches away. Carter saw himself reflected in the lenses of Harry's glasses, then watched as Harry licked his lips. His heart pounded and a sudden flush made his palms sweat.

"That would require interest." Carter's voice was just above a whisper.

"Oh, there's definitely interest."

Harry left the seat and dropped to one knee in the aisle. His torso was so long he was at the perfect height when he finally leaned in for a kiss. It started out soft and light, as if Harry sought permission to continue. White heat coursed through Carter and gathered into a ball of want and need in the center of his chest. He returned the kiss, and then parted his lips to allow Harry's tongue to enter.

The kiss deepened quickly. Harry put a hand along the side of Carter's face, his palm warm and soft. Carter wanted to feel Harry's hands all over his body: on his chest, tracing over his hips, gently sliding down his back, gripping his cock tight, and clutching the bottom of Carter's feet to hold his legs up as he fucked him.

Before he realized it, Carter moaned, and Harry echoed it as if some kind of erotic call and response. Carter lost track of time and place. All that existed was Harry's mouth and tongue. All he felt was the ache of longing to take this someplace more private.

Harry pulled back. His eyes were hooded and glassy, lips bruised and glistening.

"Hi," Harry whispered and smiled.

"Hi back," Carter said, his voice husky, and a smile he couldn't fight on his well-kissed lips.

"So, I kind of like you," Harry said. "And I'd like to ask you out."

"Yeah? Okay."

"Yeah? Good."

Harry leaned in for another long, searing kiss. Carter's brain fizzled and sparked, threatening to shut down. When they parted again, Harry put his hands on Carter's knees and said, "I could do this all day and night, but I should get back inside and check on Lizzie."

"Dizzy Frizzy Lizzie," Carter said with a sigh. "Still a pain in my ass."

Harry pushed to his feet. "You coming back inside?"

"You kidding?" Carter followed him down the shuttle's aisle. "I wouldn't miss this for the world."

∼

LIZZIE MATERIALIZED out of the crowd like something from a nightmare. She'd started the Cupid Crawl with her hair wound into an updo that bordered on a beehive. Now, a large chunk of it had come loose and reverted to its natural state of corkscrew frizz. Her eyes were glassy from way too much booze, and mascara had smeared underneath, making her look like a raccoon about to go rabid.

Carter nearly screamed at the sight of her. Instead, he muttered, "Jesus H. Christ in a crocheted poncho."

Harry stepped up to Lizzie, his expression concerned. "Lizzie? You okay?"

Lizzie slowly lifted her gaze and squinted at him. Recognition kicked in a moment later and she smiled. "Harry."

She slapped a hand against his cheek and the effort made her lose her balance. Harry put an arm around her waist and barely managed to keep her from falling to the floor.

"You have had way too much to drink," Harry said.

"You shut up!" Lizzie slurred. "You're not the boss of me." She turned her head and blinked as she tried to focus on Carter. "Is that Farter?"

"He doesn't like to be called that," Harry said.

His gruff tone warmed Carter's heart and zipped through his body to land smack dab in his balls. Oh yeah, there was a hell of a lot of attraction going on here. The denial center of his brain had obviously been working overtime to keep him from the realization. He had no idea where whatever this was between him and Harry might go, what it might morph into, if anything, and how long it could last, but he was surprised to discover he looked forward to finding all that out.

"A lot of people don't like a lot of things," Lizzie said, running the words together in a verbal slur. "That doesn't mean that anything stops or anything changes or things don't happen or people stop doing things or things turn into other things."

"Let's get you some water," Harry said.

"I don't want water," Lizzie said, her body so limp it looked like her entire skeleton had suddenly dissolved. "I'm allergic to water."

"I'll get a bottle of water," Carter said.

Harry gave him a tight smile. "Thanks, Carter."

"FARTER!" Lizzie shouted into Harry's face. "His name is Farter! Fucking get it fucking right."

To avoid replying—he knew better than to talk with, let alone try to reason with, someone that drunk—Carter turned his back and approached the bar.

Vic leaned against the bar, clipboard in hand, and frowned as he looked past Carter. "Is she okay?"

"Not even a little bit," Carter said.

"Happens to at least one person every year," Vic said, shaking his head. "Usually at the second to last bar. People just have way too much too early in the day."

"And they become so much more fun to be around," Carter said sarcastically.

"Think she'll puke on the ride home?" Vic asked.

Carter looked over his shoulder to where Harry was trying to keep Lizzie from grabbing the remnants of drinks off an abandoned table. "Oh yeah."

"I should give Harry one of the buckets," Vic said.

"Buckets?" Carter asked.

"I put three in each shuttle," Vic said, then made a face. "Lesson learned, the hard way."

"You're a prince among men, Vic," Carter said.

"Some might even call me a king," Vic said. "I hope you finally came around and have learned to enjoy the Cupid Crawl."

Carter smiled. "I have. Much more than I thought I would."

"That makes me very happy." Vic glanced toward Harry. "Any big plans now?"

"I don't know. We haven't really planned that far in advance. Harry's kind of got his hands full with Lizzie right now. Hopefully we can get her a ride home soon."

"I pity that ride share driver," Vic said.

"You and me both."

The bartender made her way to Carter, and he asked for three bottles of water and six empty shot glasses. When Vic furrowed his brow in confusion, Carter jerked a thumb over his shoulder toward Lizzie.

"She's claiming she's allergic to water. I'm going to pour water in the shot glasses and try to pass it off as vodka."

"Sneaky," Vic said with an approving nod. "I like it."

Carter filled the shot glasses from one water bottle and asked the bartender for a tray. She frowned but passed him one, and Carter arranged the shot glasses on it. Tucking the water bottles beneath his arms, he carried the tray to where Lizzie was hanging backwards over Harry's arm, shouting in a sing-song voice, "I want to do shots!"

"I have shots," Carter said, sliding the tray onto a high top table and setting the water bottles at the opposite edge.

Lizzie staggered to her feet and parted the tangle of hair that covered her face. "Farter?" She looked at the tray of shot glasses and her eyes widened. "What's that?"

"Vodka," Carter said, and handed Lizzie a shot glass. "Bottoms up."

Harry opened his mouth to protest, but Carter shook his head and glanced at the water bottles. Harry smirked and nodded, then reached for a shot glass.

"I like vodka," he said.

Lizzie threw back the first shot, then shoved Harry's hand aside and grabbed another shot glass, downing that as well.

"Yes! Mama needs vodka!"

In moments, all six shot glasses were empty, and Lizzie started dancing around the table.

"Tell me you're getting her into a Lyft or Uber sometime soon," Carter said. With Lizzie preoccupied by dancing, he quickly poured water into the shot glasses.

"I wouldn't do that to one of those drivers," Harry said. "But her sister agreed to come pick her up."

"You have her sister's phone number?"

"No, but I have Lizzie's phone, and I know the password." Harry waggled his eyebrows.

"Good thing you're a trustworthy type," Carter said.

"Not in everything," Harry said, the low and deep timber of his voice sending a shiver down Carter's spine.

"I'll keep that in mind," Carter said, and was surprised to feel himself blushing.

They managed to keep Lizzie drinking shot glasses filled with water until her phone buzzed in Harry's pocket. He looked at the screen and smiled.

"She's on her way," Harry said.

"Does she know what she's in for?" Carter asked.

"A little," Harry said.

"So, she's giving you a ride home, too?" Carter asked, trying to act nonchalant about it.

"Oh, hell no," Harry said with a laugh. "I'm dumping Lizzie in the car and slamming the door shut after her."

Carter laughed. "Had enough of it for the day?"

"For the year," Harry grumbled.

Fifteen long minutes later, Lizzie's phone buzzed with another text.

"She's here," Harry said, then looked at Carter. "Can you give me a hand?"

"Absolutely."

They started leading Lizzie toward the door. At first, she went along willingly, but once they got closer to the exit, she started dragging her feet.

"I don't wanna go outside," she said.

"There's someone outside who wants to see you," Harry said.

"Who?"

"Someone special," Carter said.

"Really? Is he hot?" Lizzie slurred.

"Super hot," Carter said.

They managed to get her out the door where a car idled by the curb. A woman wearing a heavy parka sat behind the wheel. When she saw Lizzie's condition, she put her face in her hands and shook her head.

"Hi Amy," Harry said as he opened the passenger door. "I'm Harry. This is Carter."

"Farter, goddammit!" Lizzie shouted. She looked into the car and smiled. "Amy! Oh, it's my sister, Amy." She looked between Harry and Carter with a smile. "I love her. I totally love her."

"Hi Liz," Amy said with a sigh. "Had a good time I see."

"I loved it! You should come in, too. Come on!"

Lizzie pulled free from Harry and Carter and made a break for the bar entrance. They managed to catch her before she got inside, and half-walked, half-dragged her to the car. With some struggle, they got her to sit in the passenger seat, and Harry managed to buckle her seatbelt as Lizzie licked the side of his face and pinched his ass.

"Hold up!"

Carter turned to see Vic speed-walking toward them from one

of the shuttles. He carried a bright red plastic bucket, which he handed to Harry. Leaning down, Vic waved to Amy and patted Lizzie on the shoulder.

"Good to see you again, Lizzie," Vic said. "Take some aspirin when you get home."

"'Kay," Lizzie said.

Harry set the bucket between her feet and held her head up so he could look her in the eye.

"Thanks for inviting me to the Cupid Crawl," Harry said. "I'm really glad I came."

Lizzie slapped a hand against his cheek and smiled. "Me, too."

"If you feel sick, lean over and aim for the red bucket," Harry said.

"Jesus Christ," Amy muttered.

"Thanks for taking her home, Amy," Harry said. "Oh, here's her phone."

Amy accepted the phone and slid it into the pocket of her coat.

"Bye, Harry," Lizzie said. "Bye, Fart—"

Harry slammed the door, cutting off the last of the word. Amy put the car in gear and pulled out of the lot.

"I bet she gets six blocks before she loses it," Carter said.

"Three," Vic said.

Harry squinted at the car which had come to a stop at a red light at the corner. "One block. She just leaned forward and Amy's put her window down."

"Ugh," Carter said with a shudder.

"Come on inside, guys," Vic said. "Time for the grand prize giveaway."

"This better be good," Carter said. "You've been dangling this prize out there all day to keep me on this wild ride."

Vic gestured toward Harry. "Yeah, and you're welcome."

Carter's stomach tightened, and he slid his gaze to the side to find Harry looking at him. Not just looking at him, but *looking* looking at him, as if he were truly seeing Carter. And from his expression, Harry liked what he saw. And that made Carter feel... what? Apprehensive, yes. But excited, too, maybe. And a bit hopeful.

But overall, apprehensive. Oh yeah, he felt that in spades. He'd been dating off essentially a fast food menu for a long time, and Harry, while he wasn't perfect by any means, was definitely not a dollar menu guy who would only be good for a quick hook up. Carter needed to handle whatever came next a lot differently than he'd done in the past. Even how he handled Phillip, his only long term relationship to date. If six months and stolen money could be considered long term.

In just this one crazy, fucked up day, everything had suddenly changed, and the realization left him a bit woozy.

Vic had apparently given the event a most appropriate name.

Harry held the door for both of them, and Carter smiled as he walked past. As Vic headed for the deejay booth, Carter and Harry found an open spot by the bar. Carter told his stubborn mind to stop overthinking things and just enjoy the moment. He really needed to stop his spinning thoughts and simply talk with Harry.

He turned with that intention, but then the music quieted and Vic's voice boomed through the sound system.

"Hello, Crawlers! How's everyone doing?"

CHAPTER ELEVEN

"Did you all have a good time today?" Vic asked.

Everyone cheered, Carter and Harry included.

"Excellent, I'm glad to hear it. So we're at the end of the Cupid Crawl—"

A chorus of boos drowned him out, and he laughed as he held up a hand.

"I know," Vic said. "I'm sad about it, too. The good news is, you don't have to go home yet."

Cheers and whistles.

"Exactly," Vic said. "We've got a couple bits of business to finish up before I declare this year's Cupid Crawl officially completed. First of all, a few minutes after these final giveaways, the shuttles will be leaving to return to That Corner Bar where we started our journey today. If you have a car or driver waiting for you back at the first bar, be sure you're on the shuttles a few minutes after the prize giveaways. Also, if you left anything on the shuttle, a coat, a hoodie, anything else, and you're not returning to the first bar, make sure you get your stuff before the shuttles leave."

"I think I left my dignity on one!" a guy in the crowd shouted, and everyone laughed.

"If you can find it again, you'd better go grab it," Vic said, which prompted more laughter. He held up the manila envelope and shook it. "Drawing time! Since we left Minor Chords early—"

"That fucking place sucked!" someone shouted.

"Now, now," Vic said, but with a grin. "They had no idea they would get that busy today. But, since we left there early, I'm going to do two drawings. This first one is for that prize, which is pretty awesome. It includes a one hundred dollar Visa gift card and a one hundred dollar gift certificate to TicketMaster, so you can go see a concert and buy some refreshments."

"Damn," Carter said, and exchanged an impressed look with Harry as they both dug their tickets from their pockets. "That's a pretty sweet gift."

"Yeah, it is," Harry said. "Although that TicketMaster gift certificate would probably only cover the service fees."

"All right, are you ready?" Vic said into the microphone, and was answered by a loud chorus of "Yeah!"

Vic drew a ticket from the envelope and read off the number. A woman standing near Carter let out a scream loud enough to make him jump, and then she ran up to the deejay booth as her friends cheered and screamed for her. Vic checked her ticket then handed over the prizes and the woman danced her way back to her friends as everyone else applauded.

"Now we're up to the final prize of the day," Vic said. "This is a pretty amazing prize, if I do say so myself. How many of you here know a singer named Rex Garland?"

Carter laughed as a good number of the crowd cheered, and men and women alike catcalled.

"What's so funny?" Harry asked, leaning down to speak into his ear.

"My best friend is married to Rex!" Carter explained.

"Seriously?"

"Seriously!"

"Yeah, Rex is pretty hot," Vic said into the microphone. "I gotta admit it. In his early days, he used to perform right here in this bar."

Carter had never heard Rex say anything about singing at Cheeky Monkey, and he shrugged at Harry's inquisitive look. He was definitely going to have to ask Rex about that when he and Will returned.

"So, based on a generous donation from Gail Dumont, the owner of this fine establishment, we have a grand prize you're going to love. Are you all familiar with Rex's Christmas song?"

"Can I Pretend You're Mine for Christmas?" a few people shouted back, Carter included.

"Right! Do you know the story of how it was written?" Vic said.

A good number of people cheered, and Carter laughed and nodded. He'd had a front row seat to the craziness around Rex's efforts to write the song and Will leaving Rex secret notes containing lyrics.

"Well, it all happened at a hotel in upstate New York called the Williamsville Inn. And this prize pack includes a four day, three night stay at the newly remodeled Williamsville Inn. How's that sound?"

Carter clapped and cheered along with everyone else, exchanging a smile with Harry.

"All right, for the final prize of the day, get your tickets ready." Vic vigorously shook the manila envelope for a full minute before slipping his hand inside and pulling out a ticket. "And the winner of the Williamsville Inn weekend getaway is…"

Vic read off a number.

Carter stared at his ticket.

No. Really?

THE CUPID CRAWL

Had he just won a goddamn weekend trip to the hotel where Will and Rex had met and written a hit Christmas song together?

"Is there a winner?" Vic asked, looking around the crowd.

Carter couldn't speak. All he could do was stare at his ticket. How in the hell had this happened? What kind of circumstance and luck had come together for him to not only meet an amazing man at this crazy bar crawl, but also win a stay at the place that had changed his best friend's life?

"You won!" Harry shouted, and grabbed Carter by the shoulders. "Here! Carter won!"

"Really? Carter?" Vic laughed as everyone cheered. "Come on up here, Carter!"

People clapped him on the back and shoulders as he headed toward Vic. Quite a few smacked him on the ass, and he laughed each time. Was this really happening?

When he reached Vic, he was surprised by the bear hug he received. Vic beamed as he moved back, and everyone from the Cupid Crawl was clapping and whooping. Even Ivy, who stood way off to the side, her black feathered wings shaking with the force of her claps, and her smile big and bright in her pale face.

"Congratulations on being our big winner," Vic said into the microphone. "Do you know who Rex Garland is?"

Vic held the microphone toward him and Carter said into it, "Um, yeah, I know Rex. He's actually married to my best friend."

More cheers, clapping, and an annoyingly piercing whistle from somewhere in the back of the crowd.

"Are you serious?" Vic asked.

"Yeah, totally serious."

"So you know the Williamsville Inn?" Vic asked.

"I wasn't there, but Will, my friend Rex is married to, stayed there on one of his business trips. He would FaceTime with me, and told me about Rex being there and the notes with lyrics he left for him in the courtyard. I was best man at their wedding this past New Year's Eve."

Amid the cheers and clapping, Vic handed Carter an envelope. He squeezed Carter's shoulder and smiled at him.

"Congratulations, Carter."

"Thanks, Vic."

"It's been a pleasure getting to know you."

"It's been an interesting day," Carter said. "I'm glad I came. And not just because of this." He held up the envelope.

Vic smiled and winked. "Happy Valentine's Day, Carter."

Carter could see Harry's smiling face above the crowd, and he headed toward him. More back slaps and shoulder squeezes, as well as ass smacks. When he finally reached Harry, Carter discovered that Ivy had made her way through the crowd to join them.

"That's amazing you won," Ivy said. "Did you stuff the envelope or something?"

"Nope. I can't believe I won the grand prize," Carter said. "And that it's for the Williamsville Inn, of all places. It's so weird."

"The Universe is a weird place," Ivy said, and pulled the flask from her inner pocket. "I'm living proof of that." She took a swig and held the flask out.

"You know what... Yeah. I'll do it." He took the flask, but hesitated. "What is it?"

Ivy grinned. "Liquor."

Carter gave her a narrow-eyed look. "You think I'm too scared to do it."

Ivy lifted one eyebrow. "Do I?"

Harry stood watching the whole exchange with a small smile. Carter lifted the flask in a toast to him, then toasted Ivy, and raised the flask to his lips. He tipped his head back and liquid flowed into his mouth. It wasn't bitter or harsh. It was cool and refreshing.

It was water.

Carter swallowed and grinned at Ivy. "Water? This is what you've been drinking all day?"

She smirked. "What were you expecting?"

"It's water?" Harry said, then laughed.

Carter handed the flask back to Ivy. "It's been fun meeting you."

"I know," Ivy said, tucking the flask out of sight into the pocket inside her jacket. "I messaged you on Facebook with my phone number. Text me sometime if you want to hang out. Or talk about people. Whatever."

"You're awesome," Harry said to Ivy, then stepped up to Carter and pulled him close. "But you…" Harry leaned down to give him a soft, lingering kiss. "You're amazing."

Fireworks went off in Carter's mind as Harry kissed him. His heart pounded and a web of tingles spread across the top of his skull. He'd never had these kinds of reaction from a kiss before. Hell, he'd never had these reactions to *sex* before!

When Harry pulled away, Carter gave him a dazed smile. Then his snark kicked in and he squinted through one eye and said, "You're just trying to get in on this weekend at the Williamsville Inn, aren't you? I see through your schemes."

They all laughed.

"You busted me," Harry said, then kissed him again.

Vic called for everyone's attention, and Carter turned to face the deejay booth. Harry put an arm around him, placing his hand on Carter's chest. The warmth of Harry's touch helped Carter center his thoughts even as a wave of want and need rushed through him. It was like Harry had sent Carter shooting into orbit with the kiss, but kept him anchored safely on Earth with his touch.

What the hell was going on here? This was so much more than a quick meet up with the possibility of a spark. He had no idea where this was going, but he was excited to find out.

"Friends, this concludes the Cupid Crawl for another year."

Loud boos made Vic laugh and he waved them into silence.

"I know, I know. The bad thing is, the Cupid Crawl is over. The good thing is, you don't have to go home! Feel free to stay here or hitch a ride back to the first bar on one of the shuttles. If you've been drinking, please be smart and don't drive. I want to see all of you back here next year, safe and sound. Thank you for another fun and love filled event. If you're in town for St. Patrick's Day and looking for something fun to do, check out my Leprechaun Crawl, where we'll hit six Irish pubs all day on March 17th."

Carter turned to look at Harry and pointed a finger in his face. "No."

Ivy and Harry both laughed, then Harry looked shocked. "I didn't say a word."

"You didn't have to," Carter said as a thrill went through him. Was he already *not* making plans with Harry for the following month?

"All right, boys," Ivy said. "I've had enough of all this mushy stuff and interacting with people. I'm going home and hug my iguana."

"That's so weird," Carter said.

"Iguana?" Harry muttered.

"Lizards are better than people," Ivy said. "So shut up and hug me."

Carter gave her a strong hug, surprised at the muscles in her back. He smiled when he stepped back. "Thanks for being my bright spot of darkness today."

Ivy snorted. "I like that description. And if I was any kind of bright spot, he must have been the sun and the moon." She jerked a thumb toward Harry. "But, yeah, I get what you mean. It was good to meet you, Carter. Let's meet up sometime."

"I'd like that," Carter said.

Harry's phone rang and he pulled it from his pocket. He frowned, then turned away and headed for the exit, pressing the phone to his ear.

"It's probably the magician he works for," Ivy said in her deadpan bored tone.

Carter laughed, then frowned. "So you're saying he's a magician's assistant?"

"I am," Ivy said. "And with that, I will take my leave. Good luck with everything, Carter. Don't overthink things, just enjoy it."

"I have no idea what you're talking about," Carter said.

Ivy arched one eyebrow. "Yes, you do."

Carter sighed. "Fine. I'll work on it. And you work on talking to more people."

"That's not going to happen," she said. "But good try."

She turned for the exit and Carter smiled as he watched her leave, glossy black feathers reflecting the lights of the dance floor like a goth rainbow. Ivy pushed the door open and stepped out of sight. Before the door could close, Harry grabbed it and entered the bar. His eyes were wide and hair a bit windblown as he blinked in the dim lighting of the bar. When his gaze met Carter's, he hurried over.

"Hi," Harry said. "I hate to do this, but something's come up, and I have to leave."

"Oh?"

A tiny crack ran through Carter's good mood, but he managed to keep his expression open and neutral. At least, he hoped he did.

"I hope nothing's wrong?" Carter said, fishing for an explanation without coming out and asking for one. Did he deserve an explanation? He wanted one, but wasn't sure if he had the right to ask for more details. He didn't want to come across as nosey. Or clingy.

Was Harry running off to meet a lover?

Was Harry even seeing anyone else at this time? He'd been flirting with men and women at each of the bars on the Cupid Crawl, could he have someone he was more involved with waiting for him at home?

"It's kind of... a lot to explain right now," Harry said. "I'm sorry. I just really need to go."

"Okay. Yeah, sure. I'm... sure."

Carter dropped his gaze and took a breath. He didn't know Harry well enough to have earned an explanation. He needed to be okay with that fact.

Looking up again, Carter was surprised at the turmoil plainly displayed on Harry's face. And when Harry grabbed him by the upper arms and leaned down to give him a hot, intense kiss, Carter's brain stumbled through a few random thoughts—*hot, passionate, dear God I could kiss him all day*—before shutting down completely. All he could focus on was the feel of Harry's lips on his, and Harry's tongue sweeping into his mouth. This was the best kiss he'd ever received. Even better than the kiss on the shuttle just a short time ago.

When Harry finally pulled back, he kept hold of Carter's arms, and looked at him with breath-stealing intensity.

"I am so glad I came today," Harry said, his voice rough with emotion and his eyes shining behind his glasses. "But, I hate leaving you like this."

Carter smiled and placed his hands on Harry's chest, feeling the muscles tighten. "It's okay."

"I was hoping we could go to dinner or something," Harry said. "I just... I really need to leave."

"It's all right," Carter said. "Really."

And, truth was, it really was all right with Carter if Harry left. The goodbye kiss, the honest emotion in Harry's expression, and the conversations he'd had with Harry all day had helped Carter get a feel for the man. Harry more or less emanated a sense of trustworthiness, and Carter had no doubt if Harry needed to leave, it was for something important.

He just hoped that something important wasn't a long term relationship that needed some attention.

No, he wouldn't let his mind wander off in that direction.

"In case you can't tell, I'm really happy we met," Harry said. "Can I get a raincheck on dinner?"

"Absolutely," Carter said.

Harry kissed him again, quickly this time, and with a lot less tongue, and then he turned to stride out the door of the bar. Carter watched the door for a moment, half-expecting Harry to fling it open once again. But no one entered, and Carter finally turned away.

Then he realized they hadn't exchanged phone numbers.

"No," he whispered, and hurried to the door. Stepping out into the bitter cold and fading daylight, he looked around the parking lot and sidewalk. There was no sign of Harry, and Carter thumped the side of his fist against the door. "Dammit. What the hell is wrong with me?"

He went back inside, his mood deflated. There were ways to find Harry, he knew that much, but not easily. He could contact Lizzie and ask her to give Harry his number. But that would mean talking to Lizzie, and after her actions today, he wasn't sure he'd ever be ready to speak to her again.

Carter the Farter? Grow the fuck up.

Vic stood at the bar, and a surge of hope went through him. Vic might have Harry's mobile number! He approached and tapped Vic on the arm.

"Hey, it's our Big Winner," Vic said. "How you doing?"

"I'm good, thanks. But I have a small problem, and you might be able to help."

Vic turned to face him and leaned one arm on the bar. "I'd be happy to help. What's the problem?"

"Harry had to leave very abruptly, and we didn't get a chance to exchange phone numbers." Carter gave Vic his best puppy dog eyes. "Would you be able to give me his number?"

Vic made a face. "Oh, sorry. Lots of privacy concerns around that. Even though I saw you two hanging out most of the day, and playing tonsil hockey just a short time ago, I really can't give you any personal information of his I might have."

"Oh, okay, I get it," Carter said with a sigh. "It was a shot in the dark."

"What I can do, though, is give him your contact information if he gets in touch with me looking for a way to connect with you. How's that sound?"

"That would be great, yeah."

Carter made sure Vic had his mobile number correct, and provided his email address as well, which Vic asked if he could add to his newsletter list.

"Hell yeah," Carter said, then took a step closer and said, "But if Lizzie comes to you asking for this information, I'd appreciate it if you didn't share it."

Vic had a half smile as he nodded. "Completely understood. And don't worry about Harry getting in touch with you. He seems like a determined guy. I have a feeling you'll hear from him before too long."

"Thanks, Vic. After a rough start to the day, I really did have a great time." Carter extended his hand and Vic shook it.

"You're welcome. Let me know how the weekend away at the Williamsville Inn goes."

"Well, I won't be going there anytime soon, I can tell you that."

"Oh? Why's that?"

Carter explained about the heavy snowfall Will had experienced during Christmas, as well as the storm that kept Will and Rex both stranded in the airport.

"Probably best to make it a summer getaway," Vic said. "Unless you're with someone you don't mind being snowed in with."

Thoughts of Harry rushed through his mind, and Carter smiled and shrugged. "Yeah. Good point. Anyway, I think I'm going to call it a day."

"Enjoy the rest of your Valentine's Day," Vic said. "And there's still room on the Leprechaun Crawl if you want to party with us on St. Patrick's Day."

"I don't know if my liver could handle the Leprechaun Crawl."

Carter gave Vic a wave and headed for the door. He opened the Lyft app on his phone and requested a ride back home. Minutes later, his ride arrived and Carter hurried through the cold and climbed into the warm backseat with a sigh. As the driver navigated the city streets, Carter stared out the window and thought about Harry. He hoped he would hear from him soon.

CHAPTER TWELVE

The weekend passed in a blur. Carter spent much of the time checking his phone for texts or social media messages or posts. He searched every social media platform he could think of for a Harry Hooley, with a variety of spellings, but got no results. Will and Rex returned Sunday afternoon, and Carter visited with them, but by the time he got back to his apartment, he had no idea what they had talked about. Will and Rex had been too excited about their trip to really ask about the Cupid Crawl and anyone Carter had met. So he'd sat and nodded and smiled, and thought about Harry.

And that scared him.

He'd never acted this way about a man before. Not with Phillip, not with any of his Grindr dates—even the incredibly hot ones who actually looked like their pictures—and not even with Hugh Jackman in any of his movies and during his concert tour.

Harry had been the opposite of everything Carter looked for in a man. And yet, Carter now sat on his couch on a Friday evening, not even scrolling through Grindr as he longed to hear from the man he'd met a week ago. What the hell had happened to him?

His phone buzzed and Carter snatched it up then sighed when he discovered it was a FaceTime call from Will. If he didn't answer it now, Will would just keep calling. He might as well get this over with.

"Hi there," Carter said with as natural of a smile as he could manage.

Will furrowed his brow. "Are you moping?"

"No."

"You are, too. You're wearing that ratty old Henley and sitting on your couch on a Friday evening moping."

"Fine," Carter said. "It's been a long week at work, so I'm treating myself to some quiet Carter-time."

"I'm coming over there."

"There's no need for you to come over here," Carter said, but it was too late. Will had already disconnected the call.

A few seconds later, the door buzzer sounded, making him jump. He got off the couch and pressed the intercom button.

"Yeah?"

"It's us," Will said. "Let us in."

"What the hell? Did you beam over here or what?"

"I was calling you from our Lyft," Will said. "Now open the door, it's fucking cold out here."

"Let us in, Carter," Rex's whiny voice warbled through the intercom. "I'm so cold my balls are pulling up inside me."

Carter snorted a laugh despite his low mood, and pressed the door release button. He opened the apartment door a few inches and returned to his spot on the sofa. Not long after, Will and Rex entered the apartment, cheeks red and laughing about something.

Will got his laughter under control and stood before Carter, giving him a critical once over with his hands fisted on his hips. "You're definitely moping."

Carter fell onto his side on the couch and made a disgusted noise. "I'm not moping!"

Rex peered over Will's shoulder. "He is moping. But that's his choice, right?"

Carter looked them over from his awkward position on the couch. Both wore broad smiles and gazed lovingly at each other, Will turning his head to look at Rex over his shoulder. That was what Carter wanted, and he had a great chance at it with Harry.

But he had no idea how to contact Harry and see if he felt the same way.

"We came over to see if you wanted to go out to eat." Will tipped his head to the side, taking in Carter's sweats and Henley. "But you look pretty much house-bound."

"Yeah," Carter said, still lying half on the couch. "I'm kind of in for the night."

"Then it's a perfect night for take out," Rex said, clapping his hands together, and then pulling his phone from his pocket. "What are you in the mood for?"

"Lasagna," Carter said. "Meaty, cheesy lasagna."

Will's eyes widened. "Oh my God, that sounds delicious." He looked at Rex. "I'm in on that."

"Italian it is." Rex nudged Will toward the couch. "You sit with Carter while I place the order."

Rex headed into the kitchen, looking down at his phone. Will sat on the couch near Carter's head. He boosted Carter up then shifted closer and laid Carter's head on his lap.

"This is nice," Carter said as Will ran a hand up and down his spine. "But I'm not blowing you while your husband is ordering us Italian food. Especially if he's paying."

"I can hear you," Rex called from the kitchen. "And, yes, I'm paying."

"Well, there's that anyway," Carter said with a sigh.

They were quiet a moment, then Will said, "Who was he?"

Carter smiled, Will's jeans soft beneath his cheek. "His name is Harry. He was at the Cupid Crawl with Lizzie, if you can believe that."

"As her date?" Will asked.

"No, just as a friend. He's not really my usual type."

"Oh?"

"Yeah. He's older, got some meat on his bones, and this ridiculous mustache long enough for him to twist the ends into points."

"Like a villain from an old movie?" Will said.

Carter sat up and looked at him with wide eyes. "Yes! That's exactly what it looks like." He slumped back against the couch and sighed. "And yet, he got to me."

"I can see that," Will said. "So what happened? Did you guys... you know... hook up, and now he's not calling you back?"

"No, we didn't hook up," Carter said. "But he gave me a couple of kisses that shut my brain down for a bit."

"Total system reboot?" Will asked.

"For sure," Carter said. "But he had to leave very suddenly, and I have no way to get in touch with him."

"You didn't get his number?"

"Nope."

"Did you check Facebook or Twitter or something?" Will asked.

Carter sat up straight and looked surprised. "Oh my God! Why didn't I think of those things?"

Will scowled. "All right, you don't have to be sarcastic about it. So I take it you didn't have any luck?"

"Nope. No sign of him on Facebook or Twitter. Not even LinkedIn for God's sake."

Will frowned and stroked his beard. "I just had a thought."

"I'll speak to Rex's PR rep about releasing a statement," Carter said.

Will narrowed his eyes. "I can keep it to myself."

"Fine. I'm sorry. Please tell me."

"You could call Lizzie."

Carter stared at him in shock. "And hear her call me Carter the Farter again? And have her think she's the one who brought Harry and I together? No. Absolutely not. I'll track him down myself, thank you."

"You haven't been doing a very good job of that so far," Will said, and winced slightly. "Sorry. But it's true."

"Yeah, I know."

Rex returned from the kitchen, handsome face glowing. "Three massive slices of lasagna are on the way, along with garlic bread and tiramisu for dessert."

Carter smiled. "Not only are you beautiful, but you ordered me a month's worth of carbs." He turned his head to look at Will. "You married well, my friend."

Will's gaze shifted past Carter and the warm and sexy smile he gave his husband made Carter's heart ache even more with longing for Harry. "Oh, I know."

"We both married well," Rex said. "Now, while we wait for the food to arrive, I suggest we dive into an especially violent video game. What have you got?"

Will and Rex left well after midnight. Carter invited them to stay over, but Rex shook his head.

"I like sleeping in our own bed," Rex said as he pulled on his coat.

Carter shared a smile with Will, then leaned in to whisper, "He said 'our bed'."

Will blushed as he shrugged into his own coat. "I heard him."

"You get to share a bed with Rex Garland," Carter said.

Rex leaned in to Carter, close enough for his beard to scratch along Carter's ear before he whispered, "I get to share a bed with Will Johnson."

"You two are way too adorable for words," Carter said, then a yawn snuck up on him. "Sorry. The carbs are making me crash."

Rex grabbed Carter in a strong hug. After a moment, he kissed the top of Carter's head and stepped back.

"Thanks for dinner," Carter said.

"You're welcome," Rex said, then smiled at Will. "I'll go downstairs and get a Lyft."

"Okay, I'll be down there in a few minutes," Will said.

After Rex stepped out of the apartment, Will pulled Carter into a tight bear hug. Carter sighed at the comforting and familiar feel of his best friend's arms around him.

"I'll check on you tomorrow," Will said, then stepped back.

"Okay." Carter nodded. "Thanks for coming over and hanging out with me tonight."

"Glad we did it. It's been a while since I've kicked your ass that hard at video games."

"Whatever."

Will opened the door and walked down the hall to the elevator. Carter watched until the doors opened and Will stepped into the car, then he closed and locked his apartment door. With a heavy sigh, Carter picked up dishes and deposited them in the sink, then plodded down the hall to the bathroom to get ready for bed. Alone.

THE NEXT MORNING, Carter stayed in bed until a little past noon, getting up only to pee before crawling back under the covers. When he finally got up and pulled on some sweats, he yawned as he walked into the kitchen and got the coffee started. The sun was shining, but since it was February in Boston, he figured it was cold. Picking up his phone, he checked his weather app and nodded. Yep, fourteen degrees. And it looked like they were in for a pretty hefty snowfall later. No way he was going outside any time soon.

After closing the weather app, Carter's finger accidentally swiped over the Grindr app and it popped open. It had been a week since he'd looked at the app, and there were a number of messages waiting for him. He didn't really feel like getting together with anyone, but he might as well clear out his message box while he waited for the coffee.

Some of his usual hook ups had messaged him, and Carter deleted those without responding. Once he hadn't responded, the guys had most likely hooked up with someone else. Toward the bottom of the list, he came across a profile that made him gasp. It was unfamiliar, but the profile name made his heart pound.

OldMovieVillainHarryLip.

Harry. It had to be Harry.

Carter opened the message and laughed as he read it.

Carter,

I left before we got a chance to exchange numbers, damn it. I don't like social media, and I wasn't about to ask Lizzie for your number, so I set up a profile on the only other app I knew you used. Took me less time than I thought to find you on here. At least, I hope this is you. And I hope I hear back from you soon. I really want to play pool with you again. But not darts. I think you cheat at darts.

Talk soon?

Harry

Carter laughed and spun around in the kitchen before stopping himself and, holding his hands out, palms down, in an effort to try and calm himself.

"Easy now," he said. "Take a breath. Get some coffee, then write him back."

Taking his steaming cup of coffee to the living room, Carter sat on the couch and smiled as he read Harry's message again. He wondered when it had been sent, then gasped when he saw it had been five days. Harry must have thought he didn't care when he didn't respond right away.

Carter composed a quick message and had to force himself to read it over rather than send it right away.

Harry,

Just now seeing your message. So good to hear from you! I'll make you a deal: I'll play pool with you, if you play darts with me. What do you say? Feel free to text me at 781-555-3655.

Hope to hear from you,

Carter

Satisfied, he sent the message and set his phone on the coffee table. He decided to get something together for breakfast, but only managed to get halfway to the kitchen when his phone buzzed. Hurrying back to it, Carter found he was receiving a call from an unknown South Boston number and quickly accepted it.

"Hello?"

"Carter." Harry's smooth, deep voice sent a chill down Carter's back.

"Hi, Harry."

"God*damn*, but it's good to hear your voice."

"Yeah," Carter said, unable to keep from smiling. "Yours, too."

"I know this is the era of text messaging, but I had to talk with you."

"I'm glad you called," Carter said and sat on the sofa. "I realized about two minutes after you left the bar that we hadn't exchanged numbers."

"I know, I thought of it when I was already in the car and blocks away," Harry said. "I kicked myself all weekend until I thought of using Grindr."

"That was a good idea," Carter said. "I tried to get Vic to give me your info, but he wouldn't do it. I did tell him to give you mine if you got in touch with him."

"Vic! Dammit, I didn't even think of getting in touch with him." Harry sighed. "I kept trying to come up with direct ways to get in touch with you."

"Well, you got me." Carter hesitated, then decided to go even further. "What do you intend to do with me?"

"A little bit of jostle and a whole lot of tussle," Harry said in a deep, sexy voice. "That work for you?"

Carter laughed, and it felt amazing after the week he'd spent thinking and sulking about Harry. The laugh seemed to open his chest up and give his heart room to breathe.

"Oh yeah," Carter said. "I'm all in on any format of jostle and tussle I can get."

"May I come over?" Harry asked.

"You better get your ass over here quick," Carter said, and then told him his address.

"Got it," Harry said. "I'm going to take a shower and then I'll be there."

"I'll be waiting."

Before Carter could disconnect, Harry said, "Hey, Carter?"

"Yeah?"

"It's really good to talk with you again."

Carter's smile widened even more. "Thanks. It's good to talk with you too. But I'm really looking forward to seeing you in person."

Harry chuckled. "All right, I'll be there soon."

Carter ended the call and wildly stomped his feet as he shouted with glee. After that, he bounced up off the couch and practically ran to the bathroom to get ready.

CHAPTER THIRTEEN

Carter paced in his living room for what seemed like forever before the entrance door buzzer went off. He practically ran to the intercom, then paused to collect himself and clear his throat. Pressing the button, he said in a bored tone of voice. "Yeah, what is it?"

Harry's laugh came back, the sound of it making Carter smile. "It's Harry. Did I wake you up from a nap, old timer?"

"I must have dozed off waiting so long for you to get here."

"You know what would help me get there a lot faster? Buzz me in the fucking door."

It was Carter's turn to laugh, and he pressed the buzzer, then opened the apartment door and leaned against the frame. A combination of excitement and nerves wriggled in his stomach. He couldn't remember the last time he felt this way about seeing someone. Not any of his Grindr hook ups, that was for sure. There was always a bit of anticipation leading up to the guy's arrival—if he showed up at all. But right now, that anticipation was on a whole new level. A Godzilla-sized level that wanted to stomp all over his cool and aloof facade.

The elevator doors opened down the hall and a man stepped out, head turned to look in the opposite direction. He wore a black jacket of soft-looking leather, khaki chinos, and black dress shoes. All Carter could see was the back of his head, but by his height and the delicious swell of ass packed inside those pants, it had to be Harry.

When the new arrival turned his way, Carter's mental recognition program faltered. He thought it was Harry with the glasses and the smirk, but gone was the old time movie villain mustache, replaced instead by a days-old scruff of full beard. And the center part in his hair had been coaxed into a spiky, sexy bed-head style.

Carter blinked, breath catching in his throat and heart banging. Gears inside his brain and his heart ground to a halt, then started chugging away in entirely new directions. Harry smirked, and a hearty dose of adrenaline and testosterone flooded Carter's system, bulking up his desire to record levels.

Harry. This was Harry, standing in the hallway of his apartment building, smiling at him like he knew how good he looked as he slowly approached his door. The unzipped leather jacket opened as Harry walked, revealing the T-shirt with the cartoon Cupid abs he'd worn on Valentine's Day.

Carter laughed as Harry stopped a couple of feet away, still smiling.

"I made some changes," Harry said.

"I see that," Carter said.

"But I wanted to make sure you could still recognize me, so I wore the same T-shirt."

"That was thoughtful of you," Carter said. He stared up at Harry's face, taking in the changes and wondering when his brain might kick back into gear. "Did you get some help with the new look?"

"My daughters," Harry said. "They were more than happy to

help. They've been pestering me to get rid of my mustache for years."

"I'll need to thank them." Carter panicked a bit as he realized that made him sound like he was already making future plans for them that somehow involved Harry's daughters. He didn't want to come across as clingy or stalkery, so he quickly added, "I mean, if I ever meet them."

Harry took a step closer, his gaze intense and voice low as he said, "I'd like for you to meet them."

"Well," Carter managed to say after swallowing hard. "That's settled then."

Harry flicked his gaze up to look over Carter's head. "Were you thinking of inviting me in?"

"You realize that made you sound like a vampire, right?"

"It's a partially sunny afternoon. I would have turned to dust on the way here." Harry lowered his voice to something close to a growl. "And I promise not to draw blood when I bite."

Carter's stomach knotted and his cock took even more of an interest in the situation. He cleared his throat as a blush heated his cheeks, then stepped back and waved for Harry to enter. "Please, come in."

Harry smelled so good when he stepped past that Carter closed his eyes and drew in a deep breath. When he opened them again, Harry stood in the living room, looking around and nodding as if it matched what he'd expected. Carter decided he liked how Harry looked in his apartment. It seemed Harry took up just enough of the lonely emptiness without encroaching on Carter's personal space.

"May I take your coat?" Carter offered.

"Sure. Thanks."

Carter closed and locked his apartment door, then took the coat and hung it in the closet, surreptitiously inhaling the woodsy, spicy scent from the collar. Goddamn, had this Harry been at the Cupid Crawl the entire time? Had Carter really been that thrown by the mustache and center-parted hair?

"So this is Casa Walsh," Harry said.

"It is. Is it everything you dreamed it would be?"

Harry fixed him with an intense look. "And more."

Carter forced himself to look away. This was definitely different from a Grindr hook up, which was ironic because Grindr had been the only way Harry had been able to get in touch with him. Having Harry finally standing in his apartment was important, and Carter's brain and heart seemed to be at war. His heart wanted him to mark the moment as romantically significant, imprint all the minute details within him so the memory would be clear for the rest of his life. His brain, however, seemed to want to keep him from thinking too much about what it all might mean, and just enjoy what was happening.

He decided to listen to his brain, for now. His heart needed to hang out and watch like a creepy voyeur. With that out of the way, Carter focused on Harry.

"Would you care for something to drink?" Carter asked.

Harry shook his head and slowly approached, stopping with a couple of feet between them. "No. What I'd like is to kiss you. Would that be all right?"

Polite on top of all this masculine sex appeal. Romance surged within his heart and washed through his body, but Carter forced himself to remain calm. Still, he didn't trust his voice to remain steady if he spoke, so he smiled and nodded.

Harry put his arms around Carter and pulled him in close. Being held like that made him feel safe and protected, and when Harry's hand cupped the back of his skull, Carter sighed. All of his muscles seemed to relax at once, and if Harry hadn't been holding him tight, Carter thought he quite possibly would have collapsed in a heap.

Then Harry kissed him.

It was gentle, at first. A brushing of their lips. But the kiss quickly escalated into an explosion of passion. Harry's tongue pushed past Carter's lips to twist and roll with his own. They moaned together, and Harry slid his hands down Carter's back to grip each buttock and pull him tight against his body.

Heat curled into a hard, tight ball low in Carter's belly. Want and need seemed to have condensed in that spot, and when Harry sucked on Carter's tongue, that condensed ball exploded in a burst of lust that sent tingles to the tips of his fingers and toes. Hell, Carter thought he might have even felt it in the ends of his hair!

When Harry finally pulled back, he kept his erection pressed against Carter's hip, and cradled Carter's cheek in the palm of one hand.

"Bedroom?" Harry asked.

Carter managed a shaky smile. "That's not usually part of the standard tour of Casa Walsh."

Harry grinned. "Any chance I might get an upgrade?"

Pressing his hand against the long, hard line of Harry's cock, Carter looked away as if contemplating. After a few seconds—which felt more like minutes, even to him—he smiled at Harry again. "Management has approved your upgrade."

He took Harry by the hand and led him down the short hallway to his bedroom. At the side of his king-sized bed, he turned for another hot and heavy kiss. They attempted to keep kissing as they kicked off their shoes and undressed each other, but finally had to separate far enough to see what they were doing. Harry removed his glasses, still steamed up from their kissing, and set them on the nightstand. He reached over and undid the buttons of Carter's shirt as Carter unbuckled Harry's belt and worked on the fastener and zipper of his pants.

Harry wore blue cotton briefs, the head of his cock peeking

out from beneath the elastic waistband. Carter took hold of the top quarter and ran his thumb in a circle around the soft tip, slick with pre-cum. The heat of his dick seared into Carter's skin as if branding him, and he ached to discover how he tasted.

"I've been hard and wet since we kissed in that shuttle," Harry said between kisses.

"The whole week?" Carter managed. "You didn't jerk off?"

Harry leaned back and peeled off his T-shirt, exposing a broad, hairy chest and a small paunch of belly that seemed to work for rather than against him.

Harry patted his belly self-consciously. "I've been eating out a lot lately, let myself go a bit."

Carter put his hands to either side of Harry's belly, feeling the muscles quiver beneath his touch. He wondered if Harry had been with guys in the past who had avoided his abdomen, or if Harry preferred not to be touched in that area. Either way, Carter wanted to touch every part of him. He liked the feeling of skin on skin.

Meeting Harry's gaze, Carter said, "You look good to me."

The expression of relief on Harry's face nearly made Carter tear up. To distract them both, he stood on his toes, stretching up for a kiss as he kept his hands on the sides of Harry's belly.

He'd been with men of all different body types. Muscle gods, lean swimmer types, otters, bears, and the occasional twink. Harry was like a mix of all of them, cobbled together into one delicious man just to please Carter. After the kiss, he stepped back and looked him up and down. His pants were puddled around his ankles, dark socks pulled halfway up his hairy calves. The elastic of his blue briefs, smudged in different places by pre-cum, had released what looked to be half of Harry's cock, and Carter licked his lips. He couldn't wait to get it in his mouth.

A nervous flutter in his belly tried to make its way into his head, make him second guess this encounter. But the nervousness didn't make it very far, pushed back, he expected by his heart, long starved for affection, and his carnal cravings in dire need of satisfaction.

"I had my girls all week," Harry said, bringing Carter back to the moment. "I didn't get much time to myself."

Carter stepped in for another quick kiss, squeezing Harry's erection through his briefs. "Poor mistreated Harry."

"So mistreated," Harry agreed. "You have no idea how mistreated I've been."

"How about I try to make it up to you?"

Carter sat on the edge of the bed and peeled off his socks, then stood and shucked his own briefs. Naked, he slowly stroked himself as Harry looked him over, eyes shining. The intensity of the expression on Harry's face scared and excited him. He couldn't recall any other guy looking at him that way before.

"Oh my fucking God," Harry whispered, his wide-eyed gaze crawling up and down Carter's body. "You're more beautiful than I imagined."

Carter blushed and, feeling a nervous need to busy himself, turned away to pull down the sheets. No one had ever called him beautiful before, he knew that for a fact. And he also knew this was no ordinary hook up. This encounter was going to mean something, and he needed to be present and connected and enjoy it. He needed to get out of his own head.

He slid beneath the covers and turned back in time to see Harry nearly topple over as he peeled off his sock. They laughed together, and that helped release a bit of the tension coiled in Carter's belly.

Very rarely did he ever laugh with his sexual partners.

Harry regained his balance and, staring at Carter, slowly pushed his briefs down and exposed his dick.

His huge, thick dick.

Carter gaped at it and caught himself licking his lips.

"You grow up by a nuclear plant?" Carter asked.

Harry laughed and shook his dick at him. "Think you'll find something to do with this?"

"Yeah, I think I can find something to do with it all right."

Carter stretched out on his stomach across the bed. He slid to the edge of the mattress and took hold of Harry's dick. Running his tongue slowly from the base to the tip, he planted a kiss on the top before softly sucking on the head. The briny taste of pre-cum burst across his tongue and he closed his eyes to savor it.

"Oh, Carter," Harry whispered.

Carter slowly took more of Harry's cock into his mouth, backing off before taking a little more. Not only was it long, but it had girth, too. He backed off again, ran his tongue around the head, lapping up the slick pre-cum, and then, finally, took him all the way into his throat. Harry grunted and leaned over him, big hands kneading Carter's ass and spreading it apart to expose his hole. As Carter sucked Harry with a steady rhythm, Harry worked Carter's buttocks, then slowly massaged his way up Carter's spine to his shoulders.

An ass and back massage from a guy he was sucking? Yet another new experience for Carter, and more proof Harry was more than just any other guy.

Forcing himself to pay attention to what he was doing, he took hold of Harry's dick and stroked in time with his sucking. He steadily increased his speed until Harry finally grabbed his head to make him stop and eased himself from between Carter's lips. Carter extended his tongue to cushion his dick and looked up along Harry's torso to meet his gaze. Harry's eyes were fully dilated, and he ran the tip of his tongue across his lips as he looked down at Carter.

"You had me close," Harry said with a breathy laugh. "But I don't want to come yet."

Another difference from Carter's usual Grindr hook ups. Most of them were in a rush to come and then go. But Harry wanted to savor things. Wanted to savor being with him.

Harry lay on his side across the bed then nudged Carter's hip to get him to roll to his side, too. Carter shifted position until he laid face-to-crotch, and took Harry's dick in his mouth once more. Harry ran the flat of his tongue up the length of Carter's cock, his hand cupping Carter's balls. He sucked on the head, then slowly licked down to the root and back to the tip before taking him into the warm, wet heat of his mouth.

Carter ran his tongue around the tip of Harry's dick, then dragged it slowly down the shaft. Harry planted a foot on the mattress, lifting his leg and providing better access to his balls. Carter licked and sucked each one, then took both into his mouth, continuing to slowly stroke Harry's dick.

It wasn't long before Harry rolled away from Carter and pushed up to his knees on the bed. He gripped Carter's hips and pulled him around, Carter laughing as he spun on the sheets until he lay with his head right beneath the pillows. His laughter evaporated when he caught sight of the serious expression on Harry's face as he ran his hands up and down Carter's torso.

"Goddamn, but you're beautiful," Harry whispered.

Carter blushed. "You keep saying that."

"Does it bother you?"

"Well, no, but I don't think I'd use that word."

Harry lay on top of him, putting his weight on his elbows as he stared into Carter's eyes. "Should I stop saying it? I don't want to freak you out."

Carter could only look at Harry a moment before turning away. "I'm not freaked out."

"He says as he looks away," Harry murmured, then gently gripped Carter's chin and turned his head so he could look into his eyes. "I'll stop saying it, if you want me to."

Carter licked his lips and shook his head slightly. "It's not you saying it that scares me. It's the fact that I like it so much."

There, he'd said it. He'd come right out said how he was feeling, and now he'd see where that took them. Because the truth of it all was, he liked how attentive and complimentary Harry was about this thing between them. It made Carter feel he wasn't in it alone, that he wasn't imagining the intensity of their connection.

Harry's smile went from minor wattage to major in the space of a heartbeat, and he gave Carter a deep, soul-searing kiss that stole his breath and sent a shock of desire straight to his already throbbing cock.

Harry pulled back only far enough to be able to speak, his lips brushing Carter's as he said, "You are beautiful. And I'll be happy to be the one to keep reminding you of it for as long as you want me to."

A tiny bubble of panic tried to grow inside Carter's chest, but he refused to give it any attention. Instead, he focused on Harry, stroking the stubble on his cheek as they kissed. The kisses were sweet and soft, Harry just touching his tongue to Carter's. Then he moved his lips to Carter's ear and slid the tip of his tongue inside. From there, Harry moved to the side of his neck, kissing and sucking gently.

"You do things to me," Harry whispered, then ran his tongue along Carter's skin to place a kiss in the hollow of his throat. "You light me up, and make me think about doing things to you. I want to make you moan like you've never moaned before. I want your toes to curl and your heart to pound and your breath to stop in your throat. And I want you to feel what we've done together for hours after we're through. For days. And I want you to think about the filthy, dirty things we do together when you're at work, and you get so distracted by them you can't focus on whatever's happening right in front of you."

Harry kissed Carter's chin, then planted a deep kiss on his mouth with a lot of heavy tongue action. Carter's brain crackled and apparently shorted out, because the next thing he knew, Harry was licking and working his right nipple between his teeth.

"I want you to fuck me," Carter said.

Harry looked up and smiled as he ran his tongue around Carter's nipple.

"I was hoping you'd say that."

Moving up, Harry kissed him on the mouth, tongue coiling around Carter's. He slid lower, kissing his way down Carter's chest and belly. Pausing at Carter's dick, Harry gave it a few slow sucks, then ran his tongue down the shaft to kiss and lick Carter's balls. Carter sighed and closed his eyes as Harry let his tongue and lips linger on his balls. This was so much slower, so much more sensual than any one he'd been with for years. He gasped when Harry pushed his legs up and kissed and sucked gently on his taint before running his tongue slowly over the sensitive ridges of his anus.

"Oh, yeah." Carter grabbed his legs behind his knees and pulled them up. "Eat my ass."

Harry took that as an order and went to town. He licked and sucked and kissed the tender hole, driving his tongue deep and wriggling it inside. Loud, sloppy kisses followed, then more tongue-fucking as Harry coated Carter's anus with spit. He sucked on his index finger, steadily meeting Carter's gaze, and then slowly slipped it, wet and dripping, into him.

Carter dropped his head onto the mattress and groaned. Harry pushed his finger in, pulled it out, then pushed it in again, deeper this time. He crooked the tip and twisted it side to side, delivering a glancing blow to Carter's prostate that sent a shiver through him.

"You like that?" Harry asked, his voice deep and throaty.

"Oh, yeah," Carter said, then lifted his head to meet Harry's gaze. "But I need your cock inside me, like right now."

Harry smiled. "I would not want to deny you a basic need. Condoms and lube?"

Carter gestured toward the nightstand. "There. Hurry."

It didn't take Harry long to roll on the condom and slick himself up. He pressed slippery fingers to Carter's anus and slid one deep inside, then added a second. Carter moaned and gasped, tightening his grip on the backs of his knees. The anticipation was killing him. He needed Harry inside him, and he needed it fast.

Finally, Harry moved into position and ducked to allow Carter's ankles to rest on his shoulders. He turned his head to place a soft kiss on each calf, then lined himself up. Carter moaned as he felt the stretch of the wide head of Harry's cock breaching him. Harry eased back then pressed forward again, steadily parting muscle as he slid into Carter.

The full length pushed inside, filling him, completing him like no one else had before. It almost felt too much, but in actuality it was a perfect fit. *They* were a perfect fit.

The realization made Carter open his eyes, and he stared up at Harry as the man leaned over him, gaze fixed on Carter's face.

"You okay?" Harry asked.

"Yeah," Carter said, nodding. "I'm okay. It's good. It feels good."

It feels right.

"Yeah, it does."

Buried to the root inside Carter, Harry leaned down for a kiss. Their tongues curled together a few times before Harry rose up and gripped Carter's ankles. He started out slow, and Carter watched him staring down at their union as if he couldn't quite believe it was happening.

Harry built up speed, and soon drove steadily into him. Just when Carter thought he might come, Harry abruptly stopped and pulled out, grabbing Carter by the hips and flipping him onto his stomach. Carter laughed as he lay stretched out before Harry.

"I want to try it in this position," Harry said.

"Just get back inside me," Carter said.

Harry pulled Carter's hips up and moved into place between his legs. A moment later, he was inside Carter again, thrusting fast, cock prodding Carter's prostate each time.

"Oh, fucking hell, Harry," Carter said between gasps. "You're going to make me come if you keep that up."

"Not yet, baby. I'm not done with you, yet."

Harry slowed and pulled out. He dropped onto his back next to Carter and smiled at him. "Want to ride the pogo pony?"

Carter laughed and got up, straddling Harry's hips and reaching back to direct his cock as he lowered himself on it. This was one of his favorite positions, and it should have scared him a bit that Harry would want to try it during their first time together, but it didn't. It made him feel good, excited, and ready for more.

When he was fully seated, Carter closed his eyes and began to move, bracing himself with his hands on Harry's chest. Harry's heart pounded beneath his palm, and it seemed as if their hearts were beating in rhythm.

"God, Carter, you're amazing," Harry said. "Look at how fucking beautiful you look sitting on my dick."

"You feel so good inside me," Carter said, eyes closed and body moving as if on auto-pilot. "You're so big. It's like you're completely filling me up." And not just his ass, but his heart as well. Sex with Harry was better than any Carter could remember. It was as if all the other men he'd been with had been there just to prepare him to appreciate Harry.

"You keep moving like that and I'm going to come," Harry said with a growl. "And I'm not going alone. You're coming with me."

Harry took hold of Carter's dick and stroked him in time with his movements. Carter nodded and opened his eyes to meet Harry's gaze. He'd never made this much eye contact with his partners before, but he couldn't stop watching Harry's face, drinking in that stunned and grateful expression. No one had ever looked at him the same way Harry did.

And his cock was a work of fucking art.

"Keep that up," Carter said, then gasped. "I'm close."

"Me, too," Harry said. "Oh, shit, I'm there. Keep going, baby. Oh, fuck yeah."

Harry bucked his hips, lifting them to meet Carter and screwing up his face as he came inside him. All through it, Harry continued to jerk Carter off, and seconds later Carter cried out as he toppled over the edge. He threw back his head as lights flashed behind his eyes, and his entire body trembled. The orgasm rattled through him, shaking loose the last bits of the walls he'd built around his heart, and leaving him open and ready to embrace whatever came next.

He slowly came back to his senses and leaned forward, bracing himself above Harry. His cum glistened across Harry's chest and belly, and his muscles gradually relaxed around the softening length of Harry's cock inside him. They both panted as they stared at each other.

Carter had no idea what happened, but he knew he wanted it to happen again. And often. He'd never experienced such a powerful connection with someone. Never before had someone called him beautiful, or held his gaze so long during sex. His brain had never shut down that way before, and he'd certainly never wanted his partner to hold him close and spend the night like he craved from Harry right that minute.

What the actual fuck was going on?

Was this what love felt like?

"I hope you enjoyed that as much as I did," Harry said.

Carter nodded. "Oh, yeah."

He eased off and lay on his back beside Harry, staring up at the motionless ceiling fan. His brain ticked away as his heart rate slowed. Everything he'd felt seemed to have collected into a warm spot in the center of his chest, encircling his suddenly open and welcoming heart. Not only had it been the best sex he'd had in years, Harry had made him feel seen and appreciated. And Carter wasn't ready to lose that feeling just yet. Most of his hook ups got up and left afterwards. A few might stay for a while, most likely to shower or have a beer, but the majority were gone once they were done.

Carter didn't want Harry to be gone. And he didn't know what to do about it.

Harry shifted to his side so he faced Carter. He ran a finger up and down Carter's arm.

"You doing okay?" Harry asked.

Carter smiled. "Yeah. Just catching my breath."

"Okay." Harry smiled back, but he looked nervous. "No regrets? No post-coital remorse? No feeling of being trapped here with me?"

"None of those things," Carter said, and it was the truth. Harry didn't make him feel anxious, wondering when he would finally leave. As a matter of fact, he was actually hoping Harry might be up for a second round.

"Good." Harry kissed him, then got up. "I'm going to take care of the condom and pee, and then, if you want, maybe some more jostle and tussle?"

Carter grinned. "It's like you read my mind."

Harry's smile was bright with relief. "You decide if you want more jostling or tussling, and I'll be right back."

Outside the window, the mini-blinds partially open, big

snowflakes had started to fall. Perfect weather to stay inside and fuck all day.

The toilet flushed and Carter listened to the water running as Harry washed his hands. He practiced good hygiene; that was a plus. Harry entered the room and stretched out beside Carter, throwing his arm across Carter's chest.

"So, how about I be on the receiving end of the jostling this time?" Harry said.

Carter raised his eyebrows as he smiled. "You're versatile?"

Harry kissed him. "Oh, baby, you've got so much to learn about me."

Carter kissed him this time, realizing that he did, indeed, want to learn as much as he could about Harry.

∼

THE SNOW FELL all day Saturday and overnight. Carter and Harry spent the day mostly in bed, fucking, napping and ordering takeout delivery food. Late Saturday night, Harry sat propped up in bed, Carter's head on his chest as they watched a movie.

Carter moved his head slightly now and then, enjoying the soft brush of Harry's chest hair against his cheek. "You don't have to tell me if you don't want to, but why'd you leave the Cupid Crawl so quickly? If you don't mind me asking."

"Oh, I don't mind at all," Harry said. He ran his fingers through Carter's hair, pausing every so often to massage his scalp. "I got a call from my youngest daughter, Olivia. Her first period had started and she wasn't feeling well."

"Oh, wow." Carter sat up in order to look at him, seeing the TV image reflected in his glasses. "That's a lot to handle. How did she do?"

"She did good." Harry widened his eyes. "Her old man, however, was another story. Aubrey, my oldest daughter, was with

THE CUPID CRAWL

their mother when she got her first period, so I kind of had to muddle through things a bit with Olivia, but I think I did pretty good."

"I bet you did. You're probably the best dad." He kissed the middle of Harry's chest and rested his cheek against the spot. Harry resumed stroking Carter's head.

"I don't know if my daughters would say that, exactly, but I think I do pretty good."

"I was thinking you'd left to go home to your current lover and break things off because you'd met the man of your dreams." He paused, then said, "Which would have been me, by the way."

"As romantic as that might have been, it was, as you now know, incorrect," Harry said. "I am single at the moment, but hoping to find a relationship. I thought I might have really connected with someone I recently met, but I've yet to get a feel from him about it." Harry was quiet, and Carter held his breath. "So, you can write that down in your diary."

Carter released his breath and kissed Harry's chest, then reached under the sheet to fondle Harry's cock and balls. "Dear Diary, Harry came over today and we fucked five times—"

"Soon to be six, if you keep groping me," Harry said.

Carter continued as if Harry hadn't spoken, but he did gently tug on Harry's stirring dick. "He told me he's single, but looking for a relationship. If he can cook, I just might keep him."

Harry chuckled and, setting his glasses aside, growled as he rolled them over so he lay on top. Holding Carter's head between his hands, Harry stared for a long moment, studying him, then leaned down for a kiss. Carter's head spun, and he realized he was actually swooning, that Harry had made him fucking swoon with one of the best kisses he'd ever received.

And Carter also realized he didn't want the feeling to end. He wanted Harry to kiss him until he swooned every night. After the week he'd spent pining, it really didn't come as a surprise to

Carter that now he'd connected with Harry again, he couldn't imagine being without him.

Harry pulled away and smiled. "For the record, I'm a pretty decent cook."

"Yeah?" Carter slid a hand between them and grabbed Harry's hard-on. "I'm not surprised, seeing how you use your meat thermometer."

"Gotta stick it in the right spot to get an accurate reading," Harry said. "But, before I check your temperature, I want you to know that I'm being honest. I'm not seeing anyone seriously, and I would like to keep seeing you, if you'll allow me to."

Harry was so adorably formal, it made Carter's heart flutter, his toes curl and his stomach quiver with excitement. Was he swooning again? Maybe a little. And this time it wasn't even from a kiss. Where had this handsome and surprising man come from?

"Yeah?" Carter smiled and kissed him. "Let's take it week by week, how's that?"

"Check in every Saturday?" Harry asked.

"Every Friday night," Carter said. "Gives us a chance to enjoy the weekend."

"It's a deal." Harry kissed him, then stopped and pulled his head back to give him a suspicious look. "Wait, enjoy the weekend if we break up, or enjoy the weekend together?"

"Yes, right," Carter said, and pulled him down for a kiss, both of them chuckling through it.

Harry slowly lifted Carter's legs and moved in close so his erection bumped against Carter's hole. The kisses Harry delivered were no longer bruising and passionately frantic, but sensual and loving. They felt deeper and much more intimate, and Carter closed his eyes, losing himself in the sensations.

"Is your hole worn out yet?" Harry asked between kisses.

"I think it can take another go," Carter said.

"Just one more?" Harry asked.

"Let's take it one by one," Carter said. "Would that work for you?"

Harry smiled and kissed him. "All of this is working for me. It's working for me quite well."

As Harry moved to grab the condoms and lube, Carter watched him and smiled. It was working well for him, too.

CHAPTER FOURTEEN

Carter checked the app on his phone a third time, pinching and zooming in on the map.

"This is it, right?" Harry asked, slowing the rental car.

"I think so." Carter squinted as he tried to find an address on the building. "I don't see a sign... Wait, there it is. The Williamsville Inn. Yep, this is it."

"It looks different than the pictures on the website," Harry said as he pulled into the parking lot.

"And by different I'm going to guess you mean better?"

"Yeah, a lot better." Harry parked the car and shut off the engine, then took Carter's hand and lifted it to his mouth to kiss the back. "Thanks for bringing me on your trip."

"Who else would I bring here?" Carter asked. "Besides, it's my six month anniversary gift to you."

Harry narrowed his eyes. "That you won in a contest."

"And bringing you along is my gift to you," Carter countered.

They laughed and leaned in to meet halfway between the car seats for a kiss. Was it Carter's imagination, or did the kisses keep getting better and better, even six months in?

"We'll discuss this in more detail later," Harry said.

"I would hope so."

They got out of the car and grabbed their suitcases from the trunk. A humid breeze ruffled Carter's hair, and he looked up at the August sky, brushed with thin white clouds. Lowering his gaze, he looked the hotel over, trying to imagine Will and Rex here more than a year and a half ago, when the place was practically buried under snow. Based on the old photos on the website, whoever had purchased the hotel had opened up the front entrance with large glass windows and a more modern overhang.

"This is where all the magic happened for Will and Rex?" Harry asked, coming up beside him and taking his hand again.

"That's what they say." Carter gave his hand a squeeze. Harry's hand felt so familiar now, because Harry liked holding hands, and Carter had quickly come to realize he liked it, too. He shrugged and checked out the hotel again. "All I remember is a lot of romantic melodrama."

"Yeah, and you've never fallen into that kind of thing," Harry said. Before Carter could react to that statement, Harry smiled and gestured to a car pulling in the parking lot. "Speak of the devils. Here they are now."

"We're going to discuss that romantic melodrama comment later," Carter said. "Along with the six month anniversary gift thing."

Harry grinned. "Deal."

As much as he had known he and Harry were a good fit, Carter had had some minor issues dealing with the possibility of a long term relationship in the early days of their dating. He hadn't reverted to Grindr and cheated on Harry, but he had acted out, and more than once tried to break things off, only to call the next day and apologize. It had taken some long conversations with Will, followed by even longer conversations with Harry before Carter felt truly settled into the relationship.

Flash forward to August where they were on a vacation double date with Will and Rex, back at the place where the two of them had met. It had been Rex, actually, who had suggested the timing for the trip. He'd been hired to sing at a gay wedding being held at the inn—the new owner was marrying the man he had also met while staying at the Williamsville Inn—and he had invited Carter and Harry to arrange their trip to coincide with theirs. Carter wondered if the hotel might be the headquarters of some kind of secret gay wedding cult, and every gay couple that checked in couldn't leave until they got married. Well, he hoped they had a lot of guards waiting to stop him and Harry, because Carter definitely wasn't ready for marriage just yet.

Was he?

Will came up beside Carter and put an arm around his shoulders, pulling him in close against his side as they both looked the hotel over.

"You excited to be back here?" Carter asked.

"I am."

Will's face practically gleamed from his sentimental expression and big, sappy smile. Carter was genuinely happy for him and Rex. And now, with Harry in his life, he understood how coming back to the place where it all began would make him feel a rush of love and gratitude.

He felt that way every day with Harry.

"You excited to see it for the first time?" Will asked.

"Yeah, but too bad it's been modernized," Carter said. "Kind of takes away from the true experience."

"Trust me, you don't want to have to go through that kind of experience," Will said, then smiled and squeezed his shoulders. "I'm really glad you're here."

"Me, too," Carter said, and meant it.

"Let's get checked in and track down the grooms," Rex said, carrying his and Will's luggage toward the entrance.

"He carries your bags for you?" Carter asked.

"He does."

They turned to watch Harry grab the handles of both sets of luggage. Smiling and winking at Carter, Harry followed Rex to the doors.

"Well, shit," Carter said. "We went and found ourselves a couple of hot Sherpas!"

Will laughed and, his arm still around Carter's shoulders, got them moving toward the entrance.

∽

REX AND WILL ARRANGED for Carter and Harry to attend the wedding as well. The ceremony had taken place in the courtyard, the vows exchanged under an arch of beautiful white roses. Tables were placed around the courtyard for the reception, and Will had pointed out to Carter that the bar had been setup on the patio for the room where Rex had been staying back when they'd met. Carter thought that might have been symbolic, but didn't say anything.

After the ceremony, the grooms went off for pictures and Carter headed for the bar. He ordered two Crown and Sevens, and leaned on the bar, looking around the courtyard. Will and Harry stood by their table talking, and Carter's heart seemed to stumble in his chest at how handsome Harry looked. When they'd been getting dressed in their room, Harry had surprised Carter by pulling from his suit bag a brand new sport coat, a pair of khaki linen pants, and a lightweight white shirt. The outfit fit Harry well, showing off his amazing ass, and he wore the shirt open two buttons to provide a glimpse of his dark chest hair. Holy hell, he looked good, and a shiver went through Carter from his head all the way down to his toes.

That man was his, all his. He got to kiss him, laugh with him, undress him, and make love to him. Finally, Carter had found what he'd been looking for all his life.

Harry turned his head, met Carter's gaze, and smiled.

The bartender set the two drinks on the bar. "Here you go." He must have noticed Carter and Harry staring, because he said, "You guys make a hot couple. How'd you meet?"

Carter smiled. What had started out as a nightmare experience had allowed him to meet the man of his dreams. Weird how the world worked. "A Valentine's Day bar crawl."

The bartender laughed. "Sounds like a blast. Was that around here?"

"Boston."

"I may have to look into that," he said.

"Highly recommended." He dropped a ten dollar bill into the tip jar and picked up the drinks. "Thanks for the drinks."

Harry grinned when Carter handed him the drink. "For me?"

"No, they're both for me, but I want you to hang onto this one for me so I don't look like a crazy drunk," Carter said.

Harry and Will both laughed as Carter sat down. Harry took his seat as well, then leaned in to give him a gentle kiss.

"You're a smart ass," Harry said.

"If you haven't learned that about him by now, you haven't been paying attention," Will said.

Carter gave him a look. "You hush."

Will gestured toward the low stage set up near an open space for dancing. "I think I'll go see if Rex needs help setting up for his set."

Carter smiled at Harry. "I thought he'd never leave."

"Me, too," Harry said, and leaned in for another kiss, making Carter's toes curl inside his dress shoes and a parade of tingles march down his back.

A burst of feedback crackled through the speakers, causing

them to jump apart. Rex cleared his throat into the microphone and said, "Sorry about that, folks."

"I swear they're like two dads trying to interrupt my date with a hot guy," Carter said.

Harry smiled and took his hand. "Am I the hot guy in that scenario?"

Carter squeezed his hand. "That scenario and all the others."

"Wow, that was really sweet," Harry said. "Thanks."

"Just stating the truth." Carter kissed him. "I love you."

"I love you, too."

They'd said it before, months ago, but for some reason it felt even more important at that hotel and wedding. Harry had, of course, been the first one brave enough to say it, but Carter immediately said it back, and had surprised himself by not regretting it one bit. He felt more for Harry than anyone else he'd been with before. What he and Harry had together was sturdy and true, and Carter felt grateful every day that he'd decided to attend the Cupid Crawl, and that he'd stuck with it to the end.

"I'm going to be providing entertainment for you all today," Rex said. "My name is Rex Garland..."

Loud cheers with applause and whistling followed.

"Thank you," Rex said with a wave. "I appreciate it. How about some nice mellow songs until the grooms return from having their pictures taken? Sound good?"

More cheers and applause, and Rex started in on a slow torch song. Will returned to the table with a bottle of beer and a huge smile. He looked at Carter and Harry, nodding his head in time with the music, then said, "That's my husband."

Harry laughed and clapped Will on the shoulder. "That he is, Will. And you two make a great couple."

"I'm happy for you, my friend," Carter said.

"Thanks." Will looked between them then met Carter's gaze again. "I'm happy for you, too." He reached out to take Carter's hand, and Carter felt a blush in his cheeks that matched the one in Will's.

Carter gave Will's hand a squeeze, then said, "How much champagne have you had? You know champagne makes you a sappy, sentimental fool."

Will laughed and pulled Carter into a strong bear hug that was awkward because they were sitting down. Will said loud enough for Harry to hear, "And that's just the way you like me."

A short time later, Rex announced the grooms, and everyone applauded then immediately began tapping silverware against their glasses. The two men laughed, and then Erik grabbed Seth, dipped him low and kissed him to raucous cheers.

Rex joined them at the table for dinner, and shortly afterward, he sang a song for the grooms' first dance as a couple. The small wedding party joined them, and soon everyone had been invited up.

Harry stood and turned his back to Carter, placing both hands at the small of his back and wiggling his fingers. It was the move he'd done during the Cupid Crawl when he'd towed Carter through the crowd at Hip Check to the dart board. The gesture made Carter laugh before he stood and entwined his fingers with Harry's, smiling at Will as Harry led him to the dance space.

They'd slow danced many times before, often in one or the other's living room. Harry owned a nice three bedroom house a short distance outside Boston, and Carter usually ended up spending weekends there, even while Harry's daughters were there. Things had been a little rocky with Harry's daughters at first, but Carter felt like he'd worn the girls down enough to where they were glad to see him when their mother dropped them off.

"This is nice," Harry murmured in Carter's ear.

"I can think of something nicer."

"You reading my mind again?" Harry said.

"How about going back to our room after they serve the cake?"

THE CUPID CRAWL

Harry leaned back and frowned at him. "You're choosing cake over sex with me?"

"Rex said it was a Tuxedo Torte," Carter said with a shrug. "I mean, come on."

Harry smiled and kissed him. "I completely agree."

Rex sang some of his own songs as well as covers of popular hits. Carter was glad to see the dance space was often crowded, and several times he pulled Will up out of his chair to dance in front of Rex. By the time the cake was served, Carter was pretty much ready to be back in the room. The sun had set and the trident-shaped lamp posts provided gentle illumination. Carter intercepted Will returning from a trip to the bar and gave him a strong hug and a kiss on the cheek before wishing him goodnight.

"Did you have fun?" Will asked.

"Absolutely," Carter said. "Your husband is a born entertainer."

Will smiled as he looked at Rex, who was currently singing a Heart song. "Yeah, he is." Will cocked his head to peer past Carter at Harry who stood a short ways off, watching Rex and swaying to the music. "I really like Harry. He's a good man, and he is head over heels in love with you."

Carter blushed and glanced over his shoulder, then back at Will. "He is pretty amazing. Who knew I'd actually manage to land a good one?"

"I did," Will said, and pulled him in close for a strong hug. "I love you, Cartier."

"Love you, too, Big Willie."

Will stepped back and said, "See you at the breakfast buffet in the morning?"

"And by morning you mean checkout time of noon?" Carter said, and nodded. "Yes, that sounds good."

Carter approached Harry and took his hand. Harry smiled, waved to Will, and then Carter noticed the grooms standing by the bar and tugged Harry in that direction. They thanked Erik and Seth for including them in their special day, and wished them the best in their life together. The cake table had been set up near the exit, and Carter wrapped a couple extra pieces in napkins to take back to the room before he followed Harry through the door to the hallway.

Since Erik owned the hotel, he'd taken it over for all of the guests, and the hallways were pretty much empty as everyone was still partying. While they waited for the elevator, Harry pulled Carter close and kissed him slow and deep. When he pulled back, Carter let out a breath and held up the two pieces of cake.

"Wow, with a kiss like that, I'm glad I grabbed you an extra piece of cake, too," Carter said.

The elevator arrived and Harry chuckled as they stepped inside. He pressed Carter back against the wall and leaned against him, kissing him long and deep. Carter was holding the cake in one hand and nearly dropped it as he lost himself in the kiss.

When the elevator arrived at their floor, Harry led the way to their room and unlocked the door. He stepped inside and held it open for Carter, then hung the Do Not Disturb sign on the outer knob and closed the door. Carter smiled as he placed the napkin-wrapped cake in the small refrigerator. When he turned, he found Harry standing close behind him.

"Well, hi there," Carter said, and stepped in even closer to put his arms around Harry's waist. "I saw you at the reception, and thought your ass looked great in those linen pants. Are you single?"

"Nope," Harry said, and leaned down to give him a kiss. "I've got a boyfriend."

"Oh yeah? Is he hot?"

"Better." Another kiss. "He's smart, and funny."

Carter pulled back and frowned. "But he's not hot?"

Harry laughed and pulled Carter close again. "He's exceedingly hot. Like a supernova."

"Well, that's good to hear. I'd hate to think of you stuck with someone who's not hot."

"Stuck is not how I feel about it."

Harry kissed him again, but when he pulled away, Carter glimpsed a shift in his expression. It was a look of concern or nervousness, and a sudden rush of anxiety went through him. Had coming to this gay wedding on a romantic weekend away given Harry the idea to propose? Holy shitballs, what would he say if Harry pulled out a ring box right now? And how would Harry do it? Would he get down on one knee first? Well, most likely, because he was Harry and that was a very Harry thing to do. But, that wasn't important. What was important was that Harry seemed to be on the verge of proposing to him, and Carter wasn't sure he was ready for that... step? No, it would be much bigger than a step, it would be a leap. Hell, it would be like a leap from one skyscraper to another.

Were they both ready for something like that? Sure, Carter loved Harry, but was it enough to last a lifetime?

"What?" Harry said.

Carter blinked and came out of his internal rabbit hole. "Sorry, what?"

"You got a blank look on your face," Harry said. "Like you went someplace else inside your head. What happened?"

"Nothing, I just... I thought you looked kind of freaked out for a second, and it got me a little freaked out, too, I guess."

"I looked freaked out?"

"Well, not freaked out, but maybe... concerned? Distracted?"

Harry sighed. "Come here." He took Carter's hand and led him over to the bed where they sat down side by side, legs pressed together. "I've been wanting to ask you something for a little while now." He gripped Carter's hand tight to keep him from pulling away—Harry really did know him pretty well—and hurriedly added, "But I'm not proposing to you, so you can relax."

Carter smiled, and felt a little guilty as a tremor of relief went through him. But just a little guilty. Mostly he felt relived. "Oh, okay. I'm not tense, at all. And I didn't think it was that, so go ahead, ask away."

"Liar."

"You were saying?" Carter waved for him to proceed.

Harry took a breath and got up from the bed. He dug in his suitcase a moment and brought out a small box covered with dark blue velvet. Carter's heart pounded and his scalp tingled as he grabbed fistfuls of the comforter as if trying to keep himself from floating off the bed and up to the ceiling. He recalled watching one of those damn forensic shows and seeing all the gross stuff that showed up on hotel comforters under a black light, and he knew he should not be grabbing the one he sat on so tight, but he couldn't stop himself. And then Harry was back, sitting beside him once again, holding that damn box in his lap with both hands. Carter tried to think of something witty and funny to say, but his mind was blank, and he couldn't seem to remember how to speak. After a deep, slightly shaky breath, Harry started talking, keeping his gaze on the box he clutched tight.

"When we met at the Cupid Crawl, I knew I was in trouble. I couldn't take my eyes off you. And my mind kept sending me off in random directions at each bar until I realized I was orchestrating run-ins with you. When I convinced you to play darts at the Hip Check, I thought what I felt developing between us was too good to turn into something more permanent. That even if we started dating, I could never be the type of guy who would make you happy."

Carter's heart pounded and tears stung his eyes. He wanted to wipe his eyes, but he couldn't ease his grip on the comforter, and even if he did manage to free a hand, he'd probably wipe someone's old spunk or spit or piss in his eye and catch some awful disease.

So he continued holding tight to the nasty comforter, and fixed what he thought was a gentle and inquisitive smile on his face as he kept his gaze locked on Harry's profile. Harry glanced quickly at Carter, seemed startled by what he saw, and looked down at the box again.

"I was so mad at myself when I realized I'd left the crawl without getting your number. That whole week I beat myself up over it. Until I remembered you'd been on Grindr, so I created that account just to get in touch with you. And I had to wait for days until you responded to me, but once we reconnected, I was so excited and nervous to go over to your apartment. I was afraid I would screw everything up. But, here we are, six months later and still a couple, and I think we're really good together." He managed to meet Carter's gaze and lifted his eyebrows. "Don't you?"

"I do," Carter said, then realized it sounded like a marriage vow and he quickly cleared his throat and said, "I mean, absolutely, yes."

"Yeah, I thought you did." Harry shifted on the mattress, turning toward him, and looked him in the eye. "This is not a proposal of marriage. But it's an invitation."

"Invitation?" Carter managed to release the comforter and he wiped his sweaty palms and most likely spunk-tainted fingertips on his pants before he turned toward Harry. "I don't understand."

"Yeah, I'm not doing this well. Here." Harry thrust the box toward him, startling Carter. "Oh, sorry. I didn't mean to scare you. This is for you. If you want to. I mean, if you want it."

Carter took the box. It was soft and he ran his thumbs across the top.

"Open it," Harry encouraged.

Carter smiled. "Okay."

With slow movements, his fingers tingling and his brain

feeling like it wobbled slightly off its axis, he opened the box. The interior was lined with red satin, and a house key lay on it, gleaming in the lamplight.

"It's a key," Carter said.

"A key to my house," Harry explained. "I'm inviting you to move in with me."

"Oh?" Carter looked up at him, suddenly relieved and excited and more than a little turned on. "Oh! To live there, like, every day?"

Harry smiled. "And every night. If you think you could handle it."

Carter was so relieved to not find a ring in the box, he immediately said, "Yeah. I mean, yes. Yes!"

Grabbing him by the arms, Harry kissed him, hard. Carter opened his mouth and their tongues slid together. The kiss deepened even further, and Carter closed the box and dropped it on the floor as they fumbled with each other's buttons. They struggled out of their shirts and tossed them aside. Carter pinched Harry's nipples and strummed the hard points with his thumbs. Harry moaned into his mouth before abruptly pulling away and standing up.

"Get naked, right fucking now," Harry said, his voice deep and commanding.

"Fuck yeah," Carter said, and stood up as well.

Less than a minute later, they peeled the comforter off the bed and fell together on the sheets. Harry's erection pressed against Carter's thigh, and Harry took hold of Carter's dick, stroking it slowly.

"Get the lube," Carter said between kisses. "I need you inside me."

"Okay, but first, I need to taste you."

Harry slid down the bed and, in one swallow, took Carter's cock deep into his throat. Carter gasped and writhed on the mattress, but Harry held him pinned in place with one big hand in the center of Carter's chest and the other cupping his balls. Harry kept his mouth over Carter's dick a moment longer, then slowly dragged his lips up the shaft. He paused to suck hard on the tip, deep throated him once again, then finally stepped back from the bed and turned away to grab the lube from his suitcase.

Carter's heart pounded, and he turned his head to the side to see that Harry had picked the box holding the key up from the floor and placed it on the dresser. This was all really happening. Carter was moving into Harry's house, and would spend every day and night with him. And, surprisingly, it didn't make him nervous; he was actually looking forward to it.

Harry climbed on the bed again and kissed him. Carter stroked Harry's dick and smiled around the kisses when he found it already slick with lube. He lifted one leg to allow Harry's lubed finger to circle his anus before it slipped inside.

"You've had me revved up all evening," Harry said, keeping his lips close enough to brush Carter's as he spoke. "I'm not going to last long."

"I won't either," Carter said, and lifted both legs, gripping the backs of his knees and watching Harry move into place between them.

"You're so fucking beautiful," Harry said as he looked Carter up and down and slowly stroked his dick.

"Less eye fucking and more fuck fucking," Carter ordered. "Put your fucking cock in me, dammit."

Harry smirked as he positioned himself and rubbed Carter's hole with the tip of his dick. They had stopped using condoms months ago, and Carter loved the feel of bare skin each time Harry entered him.

"Is this what you want?" Harry asked, moving his dick up and down and around the rough edges of his anus.

Carter nodded. "God, yes. I really need it. Please."

"Well, since you said 'please'."

With a slow, steady pressure, Harry slid into him. Carter closed his eyes as he tightened his grip on his legs. The feeling of being spread open and filled up, now so familiar, pushed a moan out of him. Harry fit inside him so well, and he knew just how to angle his hips to hit that magic spot.

"God, you're fucking tight," Harry said, and took hold of Carter's ankles.

"I have no idea how, with you poking that big dick into me so often," Carter said.

Harry's thrusts started slow, but soon picked up speed. And then Harry pushed Carter's legs up, lifting his hips off the mattress as he got to his feet in a squat, never once pulling out of him. Harry pounded deep into him, and Carter grunted with each thrust, his cock leaking all over his belly.

"I'm close," Harry said through a gasp. "Really close."

Carter stroked himself fast and met Harry's gaze as he nodded. "Do it, baby. Fill me up. Give me that hot fuckin' load."

Harry closed his eyes and his expression tightened into that familiar mask of ecstasy Carter loved to see. He thrust once more, deep, and then grunted as he came inside him.

"I'm there," Carter said. "Oh, yeah, I'm there, too. I'm coming."

He made a strange sound like a bird's caw mixed with someone gargling as he coated his belly and chest with cum. Harry kissed the inside of his ankles before easing out of him and lowering his legs.

Harry dropped beside Carter and gathered him close.

"I'm all sticky," Carter warned.

"I don't care." Harry ran his fingers through Carter's semen and sucked them clean. "You taste good."

Carter stroked the whiskers along Harry's jaw. "I love you."

Harry smiled and gave him a soft kiss. "I love you, too."

"I'm looking forward to moving in with you."

"Me, too." Harry kissed him again. "And my daughters are even looking forward to it."

Carter raised his eyebrows. "Even Aubrey?" Harry's oldest daughter had only recently started to warm up to him.

Harry chuckled. "Even Aubrey."

"Damn, I guess all those bribes finally paid off."

They kissed a bit, then Harry looked around the room. "Where'd you put that cake?"

Carter laughed and slid out of Harry's arms and off the side of the bed. "In the refrigerator. I'm going to do a quick clean up."

When Carter stepped out of the bathroom, he stopped. Wearing his glasses but still naked, Harry sat cross-legged on the bed with the pieces of cake on napkins before him. Carter sat the same way across the cake from him and smiled.

"This is like the gay romance version of *Sixteen Candles* or something," Carter said.

"You are definitely Molly Ringwald in that scenario," Harry said, and before Carter could respond, broke off a bite of cake and held it up. "May I feed you cake?"

Carter picked up a bite of cake as well, and they fed it to each other. The soft refrains of Rex singing "At Last" filled the courtyard as Carter chewed the cake, and he looked into Harry's eyes and knew he'd finally found his one true love.

THE END

MORE WILLIAMSVILLE INN GAY ROMANCE

Snowflakes and Song Lyrics
by Hank Edwards

A hotel room with an overactive heater. A rising star struggling to write a Christmas song. Song lyrics written in secret.

Will Johnson is shocked to discover his hotel room window overlooks the courtyard patio of one of his favorite gay singers, Rex Garland. Even more amazing, Rex seems interested in Will too.

When Will overhears Rex struggling to write an original Christmas song, he is struck by a flash of inspiration and drafts an anonymous note with song lyrics. Will is sure nothing will come of it, but the Christmas magic swirling amidst all the snow in upstate New York is about to change both their lives forever.

This funny, sweet, and heart-warming love story about a boy-next-door and the celebrity of his dreams is set in the Williamsville Inn world.

Curl up with Hank Edwards's **Snowflakes and Song Lyrics** today!

https://books2read.com/snowflakes

∼

Snowstorms and Second Chances
by Brigham Vaughn

A hotel room with a faulty heater.
A holiday grump who's sure he's straight.
A single guy full of Christmas cheer.

Erik Josef is a recently divorced businessman with one goal: wrap up his last project of the year so he can spend the holidays in the tropics. While waiting at an airport bar, he encounters Seth Cobb, a chatty young travel writer.

After a huge snowstorm grounds all flights, a mix-up at the Williamsville Inn leads to them sharing a room.

Will a mugful of Seth's hot cocoa and the Christmas magic swirling amidst all the snow in upstate New York be enough to melt Erik's icy exterior?

Snowstorms and Second Chances is a wintertime treat about forced proximity, self-discovery, and a second chance at happiness that takes place in the Williamsville Inn series world. It features characters from Brigham Vaughn's **The Cupcake Conundrum**, along with **Snowflakes and Song Lyrics** and **The Cupid Crawl** by Hank Edwards.

Check out Brigham Vaughn's **Snowstorms and Second Chances**.

https://books2read.com/SnowstormsandSecondChances

The Cupcake Conundrum
by Brigham Vaughn

A pastry chef nursing a broken heart.
A single dad who made the biggest mistake of his life.
One guest room to sleep in.

When Adrian Cobb arrives in New York to help his brother move, he comes face to face with the worst decision he's ever made—ghosting on a baking conference hookup a year ago. Now, he's sharing a guest room with Ajay Sunagar, who looks as tasty as the pastries he bakes, and Adrian desperately wants to prove he can handle the heat this time.

But although the attraction's still there, Jay makes it clear he isn't ready to forgive and forget. As they spend more time together, Adrian begins to wonder if Jay would rather make him grovel or cover Adrian in frosting and lick him all over.

The Cupcake Conundrum is a sweet-treat story about a single dad, instant attraction, and falling in love all over again that takes place in the Williamsville Inn series world. It features characters from Brigham Vaughn's **Snowstorms and Second Chances**, along with **Snowflakes and Song Lyrics** and **The Cupid Crawl** by Hank Edwards.

Treat yourself to Brigham Vaughn's **The Cupcake Conundrum**!

https://books2read.com/TheCupcakeConundrum

ABOUT THE AUTHOR

Hank Edwards (he/him) has been writing gay fiction for more than twenty years. He has published over thirty novels and dozens of novella and short stories. His writing crosses many sub-genres, including contemporary romance, rom-com, paranormal, suspense, mystery, and wacky comedy. He has written a number of series such as the suspenseful Up to Trouble, funny and spooky Critter Catchers, Old West historical horror of Venom Valley, and erotic and funny Fluffers, Inc. He has also written a young adult urban fantasy gay romance series called The Town of Superstition under the pen name R. G. Thomas. He was born and still lives in a northwest suburb of the Motor City, Detroit, Michigan, where he shares a home with his partner of over 24 years and their two cats.

For more information:
www.hankedwardsbooks.com
hankedwardsbooks@gmail.com

ALSO BY HANK EDWARDS

Gay Romantic Paranormal:
Cowboys & Vampires - Venom Valley Book One
Stakes & Spurs - Venom Valley Book Two
Blood & Stone - Venom Valley Book Three
Terror by Moonlight – Critter Catchers Book One
Chasing the Chupacabra – Critter Catchers Book Two
Swamped by Fear - Critter Catchers Book Three
The Devil of Pinesville - Critter Catchers Book Four
Screams of the Season - Critter Catchers Book Five
Horror at Hideaway Cove - Critter Catchers Book Six
Dread of Night - Critter Catchers Book Seven
Wicked Reflection

Gay Romantic Comedies:
Fluffers, Inc. (Fluffers, Inc. Book One)
A Carnal Cruise (Fluffers, Inc. Book Two)
Vancouver Nights (Fluffers, Inc. Book Three)
Plus Ones

Gay Romantic Suspense/Mystery:
Holed Up: Up to Trouble Book One
Shacked Up: Up to Trouble Book Two
Roughed Up: Up to Trouble Book Three

Choked Up: Up to Trouble Book Four

Destiny's Bastard

Hired Muscle

Buried Secrets

Repossession is 9/10ths of the Law

Murder Most Lovely: Lacetown Murder Mysteries Case One (co-written with Deanna Wadsworth)

Murder Most Deserving: Lacetown Murder Mysteries Case Two (co-written with Deanna Wadsworth)

Williamsville Inn Gay Romance:

Snowflakes and Song Lyrics: A Williamsville Inn Story

The Cupid Crawl: A Williamsville Inn Story

Fake Date Flip-Flop: A Williamsville Inn Story

Holiday Gay Romance:

A Gift for Greg (A Story Orgy Single)

Mistletoe at Midnight (A Story Orgy Single)

The Christmas Accomplice

Story Orgy Singles Gay Romance:

A Gift for Greg (A Story Orgy Single)

By the Book (A Story Orgy Single)

Cross Country Foreplay (A Story Orgy Single)

Mistletoe at Midnight (A Story Orgy Single)

The Cheapskate: Bad Boyfriends (A Story Orgy Single)

With This Ring (A Story Orgy Single)

Gay Erotic Short Story Collections:
A Very Dirty Dozen
Another Very Dirty Dozen

Salacious Singles Gay Erotic Short Stories:
Bear Market (A Salacious Single)
Convoy (A Salacious Single)
Double Down (A Salacious Single)
Exchange Rate (A Salacious Single)
Finding North (A Salacious Single)
Hotel Dick (A Salacious Single)
Kindred Spirits (A Salacious Single)
Sacked (A Salacious Single)
Stroking Midnight (A Salacious Single)
Vanity Loves Company (A Salacious Single)
Wet Lands (A Salacious Single)

Hank's stories also appear in the following anthologies:
50's Mixed Tape Anthology - Totally Bound
Bear Lust: Hot and Hairy Fiction – Bear Bones Books
Bears of Winter - Bear Bones Books
Bears: Gay Erotic Stories – Cleis Press
Cowboys: Gay Erotic Stories – Cleis Press
Dirty Diner: Gay Erotica on the Menu – Bold Strokes Books
Hard Working Men: Gay Erotic Stories – Cleis Press
Hot Cops: Gay Erotic Stories – Cleis Press
On the Run: Tales of Gay Pursuit and Passion - Wilde City Press

Riding the Rails: Locomotive Lust and Carnal Cabooses – Bold Strokes Books

Straight Guys: Gay Erotic Fantasies – Cleis Press

Tales from the Den: Wild and Weird Stories for Bears – Bear Bones Books

Tented: Gay Erotic Tales from Under the Big Top – Lethe Press

Lightning Source UK Ltd.
Milton Keynes UK
UKHW021835121222
413815UK00010B/633